Praise for *Loop*

"A glorious tapestry of ideas . . . Brenda Lozano is among several contemporary Mexican writers whose playfully innovative work has met with acclaim in the UK . . . Let's hope more of [her] work will follow" *Guardian*

"*Loop* sits comfortably amongst such award-winning experimental narratives (like *Milkman* by Anna Burns, *Flights* by Olga Tokarczuk and Jennifer Croft, and the recently Booker-shortlisted *Ducks, Newburyport* by Lucy Ellmann) as a clearer espousal of truth to life than something that is, ironically perhaps, more familiar to our tastes . . . *Loop* is, quite honestly, faultless" *Books and Bao*

"Like Rachel Cusk herself, who has said in recent years that she is 'not interested in character because I don't think character exists anymore,' the narrator is fed up with conventional storytelling: 'To hell with Second World War novels, sir; to the Devil with historical fiction, madam; forget all those stories about middle-aged European men. Plots come and go, action is secondary. The voice is what matters. Listen to your voice, however it sounds'" *New York Times*

"It can be read as a lament for a species whose greed and obsession with success has made it lose perspective and exaggerate its proportions, and which now threatens to erase itself from history like writing on the sand. It can be read as a manifesto for realist magic as opposed to magic realism. It can be read aloud between lovers or in solitary silence. But most important of all, it should be read, period" *The Quietus*

"Lozano's playful prose and imagery propel the book forward . . . A delightful meditation on waiting, love, and the inevitability of change" *Publishers Weekly*

Other books by Brenda Lozano

Loop

Brenda Lozano

WITCHES

Translated from the Spanish by
Heather Cleary

MACLEHOSE PRESS
A Bill Swainson Book
QUERCUS · LONDON

First published in the Spanish language as *Brujas* by Brenda Lozano
Penguin Random House Grupo Editorial, SAU, in 2020

First published in Great Britain in 2022 as A Bill Swainson Book by

MacLehose Press
An imprint of Quercus Publishing Ltd
Carmelite House
50 Victoria Embankment
London EC4Y 0DZ

An Hachette UK company

A CIP catalogue record for this book is available from the British Library.

ISBN (HB) 978 1 52941 227 7
ISBN (TPB) 978 1 52941 221 5
ISBN (Ebook) 978 1 52941 222 2

10 9 8 7 6 5 4 3 2 1

Designed and typeset in Minion by Libanus Press, Marlborough
Printed and bound in Great Britain by Clays Ltd, Elcograf S.p.A.

Best Witchcraft is Geometry
To the magician's mind—
His ordinary acts are feats
To thinking of mankind.
        Emily Dickinson

The nameless is the origin of Heaven and Earth.
The named is the mother of all things.
        Tao Te Ching

CONTENTS

I

It was six at night when Guadalupe came to tell me they had killed Paloma. I don't remember times or dates, I don't know when I was born because I was born like the mountain was, go ask the mountain when it was born, but I know it was six at night when Guadalupe came to say they killed Paloma as she was getting ready to go out, I saw her there in her room, I saw her body on the floor and the shine for her eyes on her fingers and I saw her hands they were two in the mirror and the shine was on both like she had just put it on her eyes, like she could get up to put some on mine.

Paloma loved many men who didn't love her back and she loved many men who did, they came one after another to her vigil and her vigil was like a vela. My sister Francisca and I had Paloma from my father's side, she was the only thing we had from his family, she was the daughter of my father's brother Gaspar, who also is dead. Paloma was the only one who carried the curandero blood of my father and my grandfather and of my great-grandfather the curandero, she was the one who taught me what I know, she was the one who told me, Feliciana, you're a curandera because you carry it in your blood. She told me, This is how you do this thing or the other and that's not how you do that, and she told me, You have the Language, love, she was the one who said, Feliciana, you are the curandera of the Language because yours is the Book. Paloma cured many men who didn't love her and many men who did, she cured many people and told others their future and told them the future of affections in bloom or of affections that had wilted and turned to hate, and people liked her for that, because she was good at giving advice about love, people laughed with her and they went to her because she was good at giving advice about love.

Death called to Paloma three times. The first time it called to her was when she fell in love with a politician, death laid its egg in her then. It called for her the second time when she loved a loveless man and that time death trilled its song in her ear. The third time death called to her was when she loved a man from the city who had a disease still unborn but soon to be, and death sang to her as clear as the sun that it would come to her at six the night Guadalupe came to me to say they killed her with the shine on her fingers and I saw her in the mirror two times and two times she looked so alive except for the stain of blood spreading under her. A terrible hour, I remember that terrible hour. For me, it was six at night everywhere in the world, six at night today and yesterday and tomorrow, and for all time, and even though each place has its own clock, its own time and its own tongue, for me the only time and tongue and the only words were those ones because Guadalupe had come to say they killed Paloma. It was six at night and shadows fell across the milpa, it was exactly six at night when the Language left me.

2

I agreed to write the article about Paloma's murder because gender violence sends me into a rage. I couldn't take the unending stream of news stories about femicide, rape, and abuse anymore – or the sexist jokes I'd hear around the office, for that matter. Any situation or remark that targeted a woman or someone who identified as one would set me off, and I wanted to do whatever I could from the trench I'd dug at the newsroom. Plus, I wanted to meet Feliciana. I was fascinated by her. When I took the assignment, I didn't know any more about her than anyone else did: I knew she was the legendary curandera of the Language and the most famous shaman alive. I knew that the words she used in her veladas, the ceremonies she performed, had miraculous healing powers and I knew the stories about the artists, writers, directors, and musicians who'd travelled halfway around the world to meet her. The professors and linguists from other countries who'd gone to see her in the mountains of San Felipe. I knew that books, films, songs, and paintings had come out of these visits – I didn't know exactly which ones, but I knew they existed.

I received a photo of Paloma lying on the ground in a pool of blood next to a bed draped with a peacock throw.

A co-worker wrote me a two-line email saying that Paloma was related to Feliciana and had initiated her as a curandera, but that was all the information he had.

I've never been into supernatural stuff, definitely not fortune tellers or whatever. Making money off a person's faith always felt like a scam to me. I've never had my Tarot read or looked up my horoscope in a magazine. Someone once explained to me what a birth chart was. I couldn't focus on what they were saying, I just kept wondering how they could have gotten so interested in astrology. Someone else once asked me what sign my two-year-old was. I had no idea, so they looked it up right there on their phone, and that was how I learned that Felix is a Libra. One time, when Leandra and I were kids, a drunk with a gravelly voice "read our palms" in the park. The only thing I remember is the alcohol on the breath of this so-called psychic, who wore enormous square sunglasses and spat when he talked. I've always been a sceptic, but there were a few moments with my mother and sister that made me wonder about the power of intuition. Where it came from, how to explain it. I wanted to learn more about this famous curandera of the Language and I wanted to cast as much light as possible on what had happened to Paloma, to find out who she was. I'd like to say that Paloma's murder led me to Feliciana – at least, that's how the interview began. But this isn't the story of a crime. I'll admit that I thought I was going to make a difference with my article, that I was going to help someone, but I was the one who found help through my conversation with Feliciana. I had no idea how badly I needed it. All this, everything that's written here, is what I came to understand because of her. This is the story of who Feliciana is, and of who Paloma was. I had wanted to get to know them, but I realised right away that the people I needed to know better were my sister Leandra and my mother. Myself. I came to understand that you can't really know another woman until you know yourself.

Before leaving, I tied up a few loose ends at the office. I made a plan with Manuel and my mother: he would take Felix to daycare on his way to work and my mother would pick him up and take him to her job at the university, where she would watch him as long as necessary, even take him home with her, until Manuel came to get him. That was more or less how we organised things while I was in San Felipe. I had no idea what I was in for. I couldn't anticipate the power of Feliciana's presence, not even remotely. She'd known my real reason for being there from the first night I interviewed her, which might have been why she started asking me questions back, questions that drew me out of my scepticism and into her ceremonies.

The first things I found on the internet the afternoon

I agreed to write the article about Paloma were images of Feliciana with a well-known film director and a series in black and white of her smoking, taken by a photographer who'd been famous in the nineties. I came across the same portrait of her with Prince several times – he's dressed all in white and has his symbol, a combination of masculine and feminine, hanging from a chain around his neck – along with several photos of her with a banker from the United States named Tarsone, some Wall Street big shot married to an eminent pediatrician; I read that they had played a large role in introducing the world to Feliciana after seeing the first documentary about her life and ceremonies. In one picture, she's standing between the banker and his wife and doesn't look more than five feet tall. When I met her in person, she turned out to be even shorter. I only found one photo of Paloma, standing with a rock band from Argentina – I'd listened to their Unplugged thousands of times when I was thirteen, while practising on my drum set in the garage I shared on Saturdays with my father, who'd be in there taking apart and putting together cars or appliances that belonged to my mother or his coworkers – and I was surprised to discover, in that same search, that a song of theirs I'd learned by heart and had always thought was about space travel was dedicated to her. I tried to figure out how old Feliciana was and searched for any record of where or when she was born, but there was nothing.

3

I don't know when I was born, what day I came into the world, but it was in the last century. I know that my mother was almost thirteen when I was born and my father was sixteen, maybe a little more or less, and then my sister Francisca was born a few years later and we were the only ones because my father died when my sister Francisca was just learning to walk and my mother never wanted another man. I didn't know my father much, time passed and I heard he was hard-working, I heard he sold the harvest from our milpa at market one town over, and that at night he was a curandero, just like my grandfather and great grandfather were curanderos. Paloma helped my father in the ceremonies. Time passed and I heard he'd healed many people and when I was a girl they came to me again and again to thank me for something my father had healed, one time someone thanked me on their knees blessing my grandfather's name for the fog in their eyes that he'd healed.

What you say about your mother was the same for me, when I was a girl I had the intuition. People would ask my mother things and I would answer, the people wouldn't see me and I would answer and they would feel afraid. One time a man came to visit my mother, a man named Fidencio who sold thatch. Fidencio was sad and his face was heavy like thatch grows heavy with rain, my mother served him a plate of beans and I touched his arm and when I touched Fidencio's arm I closed my eyes and I saw a white dog near a mountain, and I told him that the dog was small, Just this big, I said, and I said that I saw a boy walking toward the mountain and the dog was following the boy. Fidencio cried and cried, How do you know, he said and I told him that I saw it when I touched his arm. I remember that time because Fidencio cried and he got angry. I already knew when I was a little girl that I was a curandera because I carry it in my blood like Paloma, from that side, from my father and my grandfather and my great-grandfather, I carry it in my blood but it wasn't until I was Nicanor's widow did I know this was my path. What is your husband's name? Manuel. It was Paloma who showed me my path, my father pointed me to it, he passed it to me in my blood but it was Paloma who showed me. I was twenty years old when I became a widow, or maybe I was more than twenty, I don't know but I already had my three children Aniceta, Apolonia and Aparicio, I took care of them and of my sister Francisca and of my mother, and then later I took care of Paloma even though she didn't live with us, she lived with José Guadalupe, her husband, and she couldn't heal people anymore because she chose nights with him over the ceremonies. Yes, he has two names. It was José Guadalupe who came to say they killed Paloma at six at night, at exactly six he came to tell me and I know because that is the only time now and that was when the Language left me.

I never met my grandfather or my great-grandfather and I have few memories of my father, but it was those three who received me when I was initiated as a curandera. I never met them, my grandfather and my great-grandfather who were known curanderos until the day of my initiation, I saw them there at the ceremony when I was initiated, I was already a widow, and in that same ceremony I saw how my youngest grandson, who is named Aparicio like my youngest son, looks most like my great-grandfather. Paloma stopped being a curandera when she started to love men, but that's not a thing you can take or give away, it comes with you, it wakes up in the night like a dog at the slightest noise. Paloma said to me, Feliciana, love, if I have to choose between being a curandera and going with men at night, and if the world's ending anyway, then I choose to get laid. And so she stopped making ceremonies, from one day to the next. People went to One-eyed Tadeo, people crossed the milpas and the cane fields and they crossed the gullies and the mist and they went to see him in his hut before I was initiated, they went to see him so he could throw his kernels of corn and tell them tales in exchange for liquor, and then later the people from town came here to see me, and then from other towns they came, and then from the cities and even from other tongues they came.

I am a shaman but most call me curandera, that is how I am known. Some call me a bruja, a witch. Yes, there's a difference between being a curandera and being a shaman, a curandera heals with elixirs and herbs, a shaman does this also but a shaman can heal things that are not of the body, a shaman can heal things of deeper waters. I heal things people have lived in the past, so I heal what they live in the present. And so people say also that I heal their future. I look at you and see that Paloma brought you here, but others bring you also, others led you here by the hand. Paloma once said to me, she said, Feliciana, love, shaman, curandera, witch, those words are all too small for you because yours is the Language, you are the curandera of the Language, and yours too is the Book. And Paloma also said once, Feliciana, love, it's not always necessary to cure mankind because men aren't always ill, but men are always necessary and good for what ails the Muxe in me, dear.

4

My mother's intuition has shaken me up three times, maybe more. The first was when I was sixteen. I'd just been at María's, the friend I started a rock band with when we were thirteen. It was called Neon, and it had no future. I had got home late – I'd been smoking weed and didn't want my mother to know. I managed to keep the lie going until she made a comment about the decorations in María's living room. She had dropped me off at her house for band practice plenty of times before, but she'd never been inside. That afternoon, we'd smoked up and I'd stared at a floral still life for what seemed like for ever. My mother described the painting in detail. Then, as if that weren't enough, she repeated a phrase I'd reached at the end of a long train of thought, something I never said out loud, but which had seemed like a hidden truth, a truth as important as the invention of the wheel. In my moment of enlighten-ment, I'd written on the back of a receipt: "We're all different." I felt ashamed when I heard those words come out of my mother's mouth and asked her how she'd guessed.

The second time was when I was twenty-three, a few

months after I got my degree in journalism. Four years had passed since my father's death, and I'd slipped into a depression. I didn't fully realise how deep a hole I was in, but I had things around me I could use as a torch. Or at least I thought so. I was at my second job, working as the assistant to an editor who called me at all hours or over the weekend to look into something or another, to write an article for him, or to finish up his work on a Saturday or a Sunday. He was forty-six, married, neurotic, insecure and sexist. He never called me by name, he only addressed me as Sugar. Hey, Sugar, do this. Sugar, do that. That was how I ended up writing several articles he turned around and published under his own name. My modest salary allowed me to pay the rent on a small apartment; I wrote for a few different publications on the side and even though I was just scraping by, I was happy. One Friday night, as I was leaving the office on my way to a friend's party, I got a call from Rogelio, the guy I'd dated after things ended with my first boyfriend. As soon as he got to the party, he pulled me aside to tell me that he wanted to break up because he was into someone else. I was crushed. Drunk as I was, I remember vividly how, even while he stood there in front of me, the idea of him kissing someone else cut right through me and I left without saying a single good-bye. I thought about Julian, my first boyfriend. We'd been together for years and I still wasn't entirely over him. I was thinking about some silly thing he used to say that always made me smile as I walked my broken heart to the car my father gave me when I turned eighteen. The car was a wreck when he bought it and he'd restored it in his spare time, out in the garage. A silver 1978 Valiant. It was like an unpaid third job to maintain, but it had a Maggie Simpson magnet on its metal dashboard that my father had put there when he gave it to me. It was a summer night, and it was hot. I didn't know how much time had passed since I'd left the party. The car's air conditioner was broken and it had rained, so I needed to wipe the windows down with a red cloth I kept in the glove compartment. I remember being at a traffic light, about to reach for the cloth, and thinking for the first time how I could kill myself right there, drive blind into the intersection with the windows fogged and end it all, just like that. Now when I say the word *suicide* it sounds so distant, so absurdly big, but when you desperately need a way out, even a flickering reminder that escape is possible – whatever form that exit takes – can offer a sense of peace. Just the thought that it's always possible to end it all can be calming, it can even give a person strength in their bleakest moments. I'd been in that hole for weeks. Months, really. When I hit bottom, it wasn't because Rogelio and I broke up, or because my workload was overwhelming. It just happened without warning from one moment to the next, the way important things do, as I was about to drive through an intersection a little tipsy at the end of a long day of work followed by a party, one hot Friday night after a storm. Something had nudged the glass to its tipping point, and I could suddenly see how dark the hole I had sunk into really was. The sadness I felt was immense. I didn't know where it came from, but it seemed to grow just by acknowledging it. Looking back, I can see that crossing that intersection was my entry into adulthood, a small explosion. Leandra had given my parents so much trouble that I never got a clear look at the powder keg I was sitting on. I'd begun to cry, thinking that maybe suicide was my way out, when my phone rang; I thought it was Rogelio and was surprised by my mother's voice. "Zoe, what's going on? I was just about to fall asleep and I got a feeling that something was wrong. Come spend tonight at home." Trying not to bawl, I told her it was over between me and Rogelio. I wanted to get off the phone quickly and not go into it right then, but Rogelio obviously wasn't the problem, all that was only a symptom. Stopped at that intersection, I couldn't say another word. Not that I wanted to. With the sleeve of my jacket I wiped a circle in the fog on the windscreen so I could pull over. I cried until I could gather the strength to drive on. If there's such a thing as a before and after, something that separates adolescence from adulthood, for me it was the moment right after that unexpected call from my mother – the most disconcerting call I've ever received. Also the most timely.

The third time was around three years ago. I'd gone to visit my mother and when she opened the door, the first thing she said was, "Look at you, darling! Pregnancy becomes you." It had been a while since Manuel and I had stopped taking precautions. At first, I really wanted to get pregnant; the idea would sometimes make me tense when we'd talk about it, sometimes it would relax me. The one thing I knew for sure was I didn't want to force things – maybe it just wouldn't happen, and in that case maybe maternity wasn't for me. I began to find that idea soothing. At some point I stopped caring, and that was when I got pregnant, in a month when the odds were slim. It was too early for a pregnancy test to show anything, and I didn't feel physically different. A few days later, I called my mother to tell her that the test had come out positive, and she replied serenely that I was going to have a healthy baby boy.

It happened to Leandra a few times, too. Once it was a lifeline, just like it had been for me. My mother doesn't like us to call her a bruja when we talk about these moments, she shrugs the occult label off like a blazer that's not her size or her style. She calls it intuition, so that's the word we use.

My mother never wanted glasses like my aunt, who's worn the Coke-bottle kind since forever. She always said they were a mask she didn't want to put on; she didn't want her eyes to look huge, like some lapdog in a shelter begging to be adopted, so she had some lasers knock a few dioptres off what would have been her prescription. I was the one who took her to the clinic. I took care of her that night, too, and during one of her digressions I asked her about her gift for divination. With her eyes bandaged, she told me there was no such thing as clairvoyance – it's just a certainty, like the certainty of fire burning your hand. With that same conviction she has sensed, a few times, that something was going on. That was her moment of greatest introspection on the matter.

5

I see people's futures, I see their futures clear because of how the Language is, because sometimes the past and the future roam through the present in the Language, but I don't see the future because I look for it, that's not something you look for. There are other people in my town who see the future, Paloma could see it like it walked in front of her and so people asked her for advice in love, they told her what was happening so Paloma would tell them their future in affections. This is something a person is born with.

I was born in San Juan de los Lagos, a town with guilt, first maybe because there is no lake there except in its name. In San Juan de los Lagos the rains barely leave a puddle, the biggest one was over there by the blue altar to the Virgin of Guadalupe, a little pond we worked hard to make by hauling water up from the river, Paloma would come with Francisca and me to haul water from the river, Paloma lived with her mother but there were no lakes in San Juan de los Lagos and no still water, no water stayed still, just like how in San Juan de los Lagos no money stayed still, coins never stayed in anyone's house for long, the rains did come which is how we had the milpas and the harvest, but if the town had much of anything it was the guilt it had even about its name, because like I said there are no lakes there, there was barely water really, just like some women have sad names like Soledad or Dolores but are always laughing. So much guilt in that town, wherever you looked there was guilt and so someone like Paloma stood out because Paloma had no guilt and never had any, not even back when we hauled water from the river. Paloma was how she was because she was born into a family where the men were curanderos and Paloma was born a man, she was born Gaspar, and one time when we were all hauling water, when Paloma was Gaspar was a little boy, Francisca said, You're like one of us girls. Then later, when she was Muxe, Paloma said, Feliciana, my dear, why ask how I knew I was Muxe from the time I was a little boy? It's like asking me why my eyes are so dark and beautiful, it's just something you're born with, like being a bruja. Gaspar-Paloma started as a curandero in my grandfather's ceremonies, as a little boy he helped my grandfather because he was the only grandson. I never knew my grandfather, but I did know that Gaspar-Paloma helped my father in the ceremonies, as a little boy he helped, and Paloma says I was there also, as a little girl, even though I don't remember. My father Felisberto a man with no guilt and people inherit things just like the branch grows from the tree, we don't understand why the branch grows the way it does and blood gives no explanations. You have your son Felix, they inherit everything, even if they've never met their dead. My son Aparicio reminds me of his father Nicanor, he makes faces like him, he gets angry the way Nicanor used to get angry and they barely met, that's the same way being a curandero passes down through blood. It's the same with Felix and your dead father who will be alike because blood gives no explanations, you'll see as he grows.

Paloma was born Gaspar so I am the first woman born in my family who makes ceremonies. I was also born without guilt, and I don't feel better or worse because of what I am and what I do or because of the foreigners who come to see me. I got that from my father, who was a curandero, and from my mother, who never bowed her head, my mother who always held her head high and worked every day of her life. She was above, not below or in the middle, she was always above and even though she was quiet like my sister Francisca when I became a widow she said to me, she said, You get up now, my child, up with you, time for you to work like me and like all we women work, you get to your feet like the rest of us. My mother lost one child to the winter cold, she had nothing to cover him with against the cold of San Juan de los Lagos, my sister Francisca and I never knew our brother, my mother never wanted to tell us the name our brother had because she never bent, she never gave in to grief and if she told me the name of my dead brother it would open a wound the size of a white tomb, red for her in the depths of her deep waters, she didn't go around saying I had a son I lost to the winter cold and that is why she never told me his name, she told me I have you and Francisca because God willed it that way, and my mother told me when I became a widow, not below or in the middle, but above, like me, up on your feet now, that's what my mother said, my mother who worked hard and never sank into sorrow.

In San Juan de los Lagos there was one main street and it was scrawny with its ribs sticking out like a dog everyone knew and I think we even gave that street a name, like a dog that eats old tortillas people in their kindness soaked in puddles along that same street we walked up and down every day. There was a pile of rocks with a Virgin of Guadalupe and a little pond we made at the foot of her blue altar and that was where we prayed because there was no church in San Juan de los Lagos, there was a blue altar and there was the water that collected at the foot of the altar and a tall stick they hung strings of white paper flowers from to make a cloak for the Virgin on her altar. For church you had to go to San Felipe, the next town over and we went there sometimes, now there's a city there,

I mean because San Felipe, the saint of the place, he let them do all kinds of things to him, they cut him all up, they cut off his ears, I tell you there wasn't anything they didn't do to him, and that's what happens when you go around naming children after your kin, they go around repeating history not knowing they carry evils in their name and so I tell you San Felipe was cut up and swallowed by the city because of its name and so now, where the priest lived there was a market there on the weekends in the town's only plaza and that was where my father sold our crops, that was where I went with him. There was no school in San Felipe, no one needed schooling there or in the towns around it, and forget about San Juan de los Lagos, which was the smallest town in the whole area, you could count the houses and the families in no time, but between San Juan de los Lagos and San Felipe there were six pulquerías that also sold liquor and roasted peanuts, and I would go with my father to buy liquor and he would buy me roasted peanuts and that is a good memory I have of him.

I have few memories of my father, Felisberto, but the memories I do have are like the sun hitting the mountain, I see him right here in front of me ordering liquor to put in that jug of his that he loved like a third daughter, the jug he brought with him from San Juan de los Lagos to San Felipe and back, he cared for that jug and washed it in the water Francisca, Paloma and I hauled up from the river and he always put it in a nice spot in the shade to drain. He liked his coffee sweet from a clay pot that gave off tame wisps of steam, like tame dogs that guard your land and bark at even the thunder and rain to guard it, that was how the steam looked coming from the clay pot and playing tame near the only window and then later slipping out. I don't remember my father's ceremonies, but I remember a few things he kept on an altar, the candles made of pure beeswax that no one bleached or painted in colours like they do in San Felipe during the festivals of the dead and the festivals of the mountains, like they paint the candles pink for the festival of the hill you see there out past the mist. I don't remember my father's ceremonies but I do remember he was already sick when my sister Francisca learned to walk and I remember the fear on his face when we realised his sickness had no cure and now when I say this I can see it right in front of me, the fear on his face when he felt death lay its egg in him.

Days before he died, I went with him to the milpa he worked with his own hands because we had no animals, we had nothing to feed them, and I helped him gather the weeds and the fallen leaves that made it hard for the good crops to grow, my father made a little pile of the weeds and fallen leaves and asked me to help him make it bigger and together we made it so big that the pile looked like a little mountain and my father lit it on fire. The sun was going back into its mountain and so the night made the fire and the smoke climbing into the sky stand out and we stood there watching it and smelling the weeds and fallen leaves burn and I remember my father Felisberto that day, when I smell weeds and fallen leaves burning I remember. It had been hot for many days and the heat had been hard, hard and the wind was blowing strong like it was brand new and couldn't control its strength like a newly born beast and the flames from our pile of weeds and fallen leaves on the barren ground reached our neighbour's milpa. My father burned the neighbour's crop and that was when he realised he didn't have long to live with that cough of his and his breath began to burn and then pneumonia put him out like the rains put out a raging fire. We already saw an ox die after eating from a milpa that was not its master's, in our town that was a bad omen and I saw the fear on his face when my father burned the neighbour's crop because of a wind like a newly born beast that drew the tongues of flame toward the neighbour's milpa, and even though he wasn't coughing blood yet he said, Feliciana, I don't have much time left. And black birds appeared and flew a distance from the tongues of fire, they flew like people moving frightened in all directions, some here, some there, and that's how the black birds flew up all at the same time and they gathered up there making shapes that never stayed still and they crushed together up there in the dark blue sky as if the heat from the fire was crushing them into a tight ball and then the tongues of fire scattered them again like clouds change form when the wind blows fierce, that's how the birds changed the form of that ball which got smaller and tighter like a fist closing because they were getting further from the fire and it seemed like its tongues were pushing the birds further and further from death, not from theirs but from my father's, which was the death that was coming.

My father began to cough blood that night, he told my mother that he'd burned the neighbour's crops when he set fire to the pile of weeds and fallen leaves, and my mother said to him, A bad omen, Felisberto, she said, but death had already laid its egg in my father, he already carried the sickness that waited for him at the end of his days and his nights, the black birds showed him the path that took him and the burning of the crops was the fire that lit the path to God. Before I became smoke from the fire that was my father the curandero, he already knew that no shaman or curandero or sage of medicine could heal him, and so during those days he had left, my father walked the hillside with me and showed me where the mushrooms and herbs grew that he picked like my grandfather and my great-grandfather and Paloma, who was a boy then and just beginning to learn about the ceremonies, and he said to me, Feliciana, in here is the Book and it is yours, it was not ours but it is yours. It will appear to you one day, he said. I didn't understand what my father was saying to me, then. None of us, not my father or grandfather or great-grandfather, not my mother or my sister Francisca or me, know how to read or write.

6

My father went on a business trip to Texas before *The Simpsons* aired in Mexico. He brought back a Bart Simpson T-shirt for me, and one of Lisa for Leandra. He told us he'd seen a few episodes and was sure the show was going to be a hit. Mark my words, he said, and he was right: we couldn't stop laughing the first time we watched the show on a little television in our kitchen that was almost always on. That was the only premonition my father ever had. *Bart Simpson's Guide to Life* was the first book I enjoyed in a household where no one really cared about reading; I had thought books were boring before, but thanks to that one I opened others. When he gave us the T-shirts, he'd said that Bart reminded him of me and Leandra was like Lisa, but when we watched the show together we realised, without saying a word, that he'd switched us around on purpose.

One weekend, we went to buy parts with him for a friend's car he was going to take apart and put back together. He'd separate all the pieces, then organise, disorganise, and reorganise them; we saw a bunch of cars get taken apart and put back together in our garage. His, more often than any other. The day we went with him, he'd come out of his room in a Maggie Simpson short-sleeved shirt. It was different from the ones he'd brought back for me and Leandra, which were white cotton with a big image printed across the front; his had a small figure embroidered on the chest. We asked him why he hadn't gotten one with Homer on it, and he'd said that Homer didn't seem like the brightest pin in the box. In the car that afternoon, on the way back, he got me and my sister to hunt for his glasses – they were on his face – and then when we got home we realised he'd forgotten his keys, so my mother had to leave my aunt's to let us in. I remember Leandra saying that it was our Simpsons moment. Later, when I started college at eighteen, my father gave me the '78 Valiant he'd bought as a wreck, then fixed up and restored. Of course, he'd said when I asked him about the Maggie Simpson magnet he'd stuck on the metal dashboard, *The Simpsons* are our coat of arms.

The Simpsons always make me laugh. They were our sentimental education, our favourite show, and Bart's book put me on good terms with something I'd never cared for. Leandra and I often compared our experiences to things we saw on *The Simpsons*. So many of our references come from that show. Four years after my father died, Rogelio and I watched a Simpsons film on television. It was one of the only things we did as a couple in the few months we were together, and even though the film really didn't measure up to the show, it warmed my heart every time Maggie showed up on the screen, and I remember that day more than anything for the memories it brought back of the magnet on my dashboard. I missed my father a lot, watching that film. I felt like the magnet was a message to me written in a code that would take me a long time to crack, and probably had never been able to before I met Feliciana.

My father died of a heart attack at 2.13p.m. on a Saturday. He was forty-five. Actually, he died from a second, massive, heart attack he had in the hospital we managed to get him to after the first one. My mother was widowed at forty-three with a sixteen-year-old daughter enrolled in open education, a nineteen-year-old who'd just started a degree in journalism, and an administrative job at a university to pay the expenses that used to be shared between the two of them. Leandra started working as a receptionist in a dental practice, and I was already a newspaper editor's assistant, thanks in no small part to my mother's encouragement when I was in high school.

My father was not a man of many words; he liked to say that actions spoke louder. When I called him on the phone, our conversations would be brief, practical. I could spend hours on the phone with my mother, talking about nothing at all, but with my father it was different. I don't remember speaking with him for more than ten minutes when a phone was involved. He hid his feelings, rarely smiled, and never cried. Instead, he'd just blink really fast; the few times he seemed vulnerable, he immediately flipped the situation around and ended up getting angry. He couldn't think straight when he was angry, he just flew into a rage. He'd invent ludicrous arguments that led him to say outrageous things and sometimes Leandra and I would get scared, but most of the time what he said was so outrageous that later, in our twin beds in the room we shared, we'd laugh about how dad had totally lost it. But we never dared to laugh in front of him when he was angry. He'd explode. And he had a hard time telling us that he loved us, he usually needed the help of a gift or a note he'd leave as if he were searching for a place to quietly slide something more in. Still, we're all capable of non-verbal communication, and I never felt the need to talk more with him. It wasn't until recently that I understood the weight he'd been carrying.

My mother is the opposite. Words come easily to her, and she has a tendency to start up long conversations with people on the street, in a queue for coffee, or wherever. One time, a woman called our house by mistake and they ended up chatting for over an hour. When she hung up, my mother had said, "Oh, that was Raquel. She dialled the wrong number but we really hit it off." We saw that moment for what it was: the epitome of her gift of gab, and "that was Raquel" became a shorthand for all kinds of similar situations, a joke my sister and I would crack with our father. That night, though, when my mother spent more than an hour on the phone swapping life stories with a woman who'd dialled a wrong number, my father had told me I didn't need to look any further for a masterclass in journalism.

My father and my uncle, my paternal grandparents' only children, had a falling out and stopped talking to each other. I never really knew why, but one day our parents took me and Leandra to McDonald's to meet our cousins. I remember feeling mystified by our physical resemblance to those three girls roughly our age. I remember watching in wonder how they moved, how they talked, how they laughed, as if I were suddenly face to face with a pack I hadn't known existed, but to which I belonged. Leandra launched into conversation like she'd known them all her life. That's how we met our cousins when my father reestablished communication with my uncle, though it goes without saying that the communication didn't involve many words. That was just his style: restrained.

My mother has five siblings, and even though she gets along best with her younger sister, her best friend, really, I can't imagine her ever refusing to talk to someone as a punishment. As tends to happen with personality traits, though, this openness has a flip side, just like the flip side of my father's silence meant that he was more trustworthy, more loyal. That might be Manuel's defining characteristic, too. My mother's strength in social situations could also be a weakness at home; I'm sure it was at least partly to blame for the crisis they'd had when we were little, and the temporary separation that followed.

My mother had to get to work, but she also needed to drop us off because the school bus had left us behind. She was in a rush, there was traffic, Leandra had gotten up late and was complaining about school. At one red light, my mother struck up a conversation with the man in the car next to ours, window to window, and the man said that he worked at our school, that he'd be happy to drop us off so she could head straight to the university. My mother opened the back door of the stranger's car for us. My father was furious when he heard. Come to think of it, I could never imagine leaving Felix with a stranger. But luck was on our side: the man showed interest in our studies instead of raping or filleting us. Leandra recited from memory something she'd read; the man was impressed and asked what her favourite class was. My sister hated school, but that day she pretended that she loved biology and let loose a torrent of facts that made it hard to believe she wasn't a total bookworm. When we reached the school, the man got out of his car and stood there with his arms crossed until we stepped inside. Maybe he was pleased to have learned something from Leandra's soliloquy.

That was the last straw. My parents separated for a while. My father rented a small apartment near his job; I remember the echoes, the lack of furniture, and the navy blue slat blinds that were so depressing at sunset, when they'd project lines across the bare floor. On Sunday nights, when my father turned on the light – a paper lantern stretched over metal rings that projected lines onto the floor just like the blinds – the whole place seemed like a shadow play and that was the sign it was time to go home. I liked spending time with my father, but something wasn't right, and I think I focused all my anxiety on the Sunday night shadow play. My parents decided we should live with our maternal grandparents; back then, it was us and our aunt, their youngest child. That was when my mother's chattiness took a turn Leandra and I wished it hadn't.

When she'd visit us after work, or sometimes over the phone, she'd run through all the details of her arguments with our father. We didn't understand what was going on between them. They were still in their early thirties, but their relationship was clearly on the rocks and each of them was an emotional wreck. Meanwhile, Leandra and I doubled down on traits we already had: I became more introverted, Leandra more rebellious. We spent just over a year at my grandparents' house, but back then it felt like many and each day seemed more eternal than the one that came before it.

I remember one time my mother spent a night in the room that she'd shared with her sister, which still had the same furniture as when she was little, beside me in the bed that had been hers. I woke up not realising she'd arrived after I fell asleep and saw her in a gauzy robe, rummaging through her purse for a pack of cigarettes. Back then, I didn't know if we were ever going home, if they were going to get back together or not, everything seemed uncertain, and to top it all off, the country was in the middle of an economic crisis. That was also when Leandra started doing badly in school and stopped bathing regularly; I remember my aunt arguing with her about it and then eventually cutting a deal. Leandra started eating compulsively and one day she cut her own hair. My grandmother took her to a salon to get it fixed, but she'd cut it so short that in the end her face looked as round as a cookie. I remember thinking that if only one of us could cause trouble, Leandra had clearly already claimed that role. My sister talked back to our grandparents and lashed out at our aunt whenever she felt like it. Without thinking about it, really, I started studying harder and trying to get my grades up as a way of compensating for the problems we were all tangled up in, and for my sister's behaviour, which created tension at home. I threw myself into my studies, but not out of any desire to gain knowledge or stand out – what I wanted was to go unnoticed in all the conflict. That Saturday morning when I woke up to find her with me in her old bedroom, my mother told me that the school had called her the day before to say that they wanted her and my father to come in, that it was taking me just a few hours to finish all the work they'd assign us for the whole day, that I had the highest grades in the class, blah, blah, blah. And what did you tell them? I asked her. That I expected nothing less of you, she replied in her gauzy robe. That phrase haunted me for a long time. I couldn't understand why, in the middle of that crisis, she expected nothing less of me. What did she mean by that? What *did* she expect? I think I began to get a sense of it when I started my degree in journalism.

I skipped a year in school and got put in with the older kids. I managed to finish my homework and read one or two books every week. Sometimes Leandra would see me with a book and hold her fingers up to her eyes like glasses, as if to say, *nerd*. My grandparents had a collection of *National Geographic*, *Reader's Digest*, and an illustrated encyclopaedia my grandfather had bought for their kids back in the seventies. I read my way through it little by little at night. Leandra flipped through issues of *National Geographic* in the bathroom; she'd lost interest in reading and thought school was a waste of time.

One day, they came to pick us up at my grandparents' house. We didn't know if my father had been dating someone, if my mother had been dating someone, or if they were on their way to a divorce, but there we were: the four of us in a car, heading home. We stopped at a super-market on the way. It was completely surreal, like nothing had happened. They asked us if we wanted something to drink, and got out of the car together. They held hands, and that was how we learned they'd got back together. I still remember Leandra saying, "Do you have any idea what's going on, Zo?"

The positive side of my mother's chattiness was that she could talk to anyone, and practically everyone would share their secrets with her. The flip side was that it sometimes made me feel exposed, as if she might disclose things that happened to me or that I told her in confidence. Like when I got my period for the first time. It was a Saturday, and I'd gone with her to work at the university. That afternoon it became clear to me that she would spill the beans about anything that happened to me, even a major personal drama. On top of being super hormonal that day, I'd just found a huge brown stain on my white underwear. I thought periods were red. I thought something was wrong with me. I was scared, so I told my mother what had happened, even though I was really embarrassed about it. And I remember one of her coworkers saying – loudly: "Oh, sure. I had a brown stain, too." I was furious.

My father was always discreet and showed his support by showing up. If I told him a secret, I knew it would be kept. I confirmed this the few times I asked him not to tell my mother something; since she never mentioned it, I knew he'd been my accomplice. Your mum can't keep anything to herself, he'd always say.

And it's true: my mother is open, direct. Her voicemails tend to describe everything going on around her in detail. If she orders an Uber, she'll tell everyone in earshot the driver's name, license plate, how long before it arrives. She doesn't keep anything to herself. My father might have been stony in his silence, but he was a stone Leandra and I could lean on. He was into photography and had an old film camera, plus heaps of pictures he'd taken of landscapes, flowers, trees, buildings, and monuments. Not many portraits, though, as if faces or people were too direct a connection to mouths, to saying things outright. His photographs kind of reflected his personality that way. When he gave me the '78 Valiant, it was his way of saying he supported my decision to study journalism, something I enjoyed doing, because restoring old cars was something he enjoyed doing. Figuring out my father's demonstrations of affection was like solving a maths problem, and the cars were just as silent as the pictures and everything else.

If my father was happy, he wouldn't ask three or four people to hug so he could take their photo; instead, he'd take a picture of a bowl of fruit, a tree, some street corner. His eye was often drawn to the thing least likely to tell a story, and giving me that car was also giving me something that didn't tell a story, it was just something he liked to do: take things apart, put them back together. The car was an indirect way of showing his support. He didn't say it with words. He knew that I knew. But it wasn't until I did the three ceremonies with Feliciana that I understood where the complicity with my father began. And, more importantly, that we still had unfinished business.

7

My mother was a widow before she was twenty, I think, and because she had two daughters and my grandfather Cosme and my grandmother Paz were poor, she decided to bring us all together to make things easier and we left San Juan de los Lagos for San Felipe, where they lived. She said that between all of us we'd bring in a bigger harvest. My grandfather Cosme was not an old man, he had energy like my grandmother Paz, they tended the milpa and the plantings and when we arrived they started to grow coffee, squashes and chayotes, along with the corn and beans they already grew to sell at the market. I went to sell at the market with my sister Francisca, sometimes I walked by the church with my grandfather Cosme, whom people respected because he treated anyone he had in front of him well and also because he looked people in the eye, that's why he was respected. Aside from working our milpa, my grandfather Cosme and my grandmother Paz tended the milpas of the Father, who was given the plots by a landowner as charity, and so the Father had his own harvest that he gave to charity, but he always also bought from us and whatever we would bring to him, he would buy it for the public kitchen at the church.

Yes, my sister Francisca and I got up before the sun came out of its mountain, we helped with the harvest and in the kitchen, we drank coffee and ate beans with tortillas and chiles, too. Around then, my grandfather Cosme got an idea to raise silkworms in the house where the five of us lived, someone at the market had told him about the worms and he'd bought some for a couple of coins. He came home that day with worm eggs and three or four grown worms like fingers. We slept in our clothes on mats on the floor and had never touched silk, but the Father had his robes, the red and purple fabrics he hung from himself, my grandfather Cosme took me to see them on the Father and other clothes for celebrating mass that were made of silk, and some that were embroidered with silk threads. And my grandfather Cosme got the idea to make silk and sell it to the Father and the landowners and the people who like luxury and hold all the coins, and so I started making silk at home.

Silkworms take four seasons to grow, the moths would lay their eggs on the mats and my sister Francisca and I would care for the eggs until after two seasons the worms hatched. And then when the worms hatched we'd give them mulberry leaves and when they'd eat them they'd make little sounds like the sound of when you step on fallen leaves in your huaraches. That's how the worms chewed, and you'd think, how could something small as a baby's finger make as much noise as a soldier marching on fallen leaves, but there they were, chewing away, those damned baby fingers and their racket, and when the worms got to be a good size we separated them from the little ones so they didn't eat each other, because that's how life is, that's how we all are, even the worms are like people, if you leave three men alone with a machete they'll find a way to kill one another and you'll never know how all three managed to die by the same machete, and that's how worms are just like people, if you leave them alone, they'll kill each other and you'll never know how the one who killed the other two died, worms and people both like to go at their kind with machetes. The older worms, the ones fat like the fingers of an overfed man, they start to drool and that's when you put them on a dry stick so they spit the silk onto it. At night my grandfather Cosme and I cleaned the silk the worms would leave, that was when we started drinking the coffee we grew and selling the silk we made, not just to the Father but also to a rich family he knew well. We made the threads, my grandmother coloured them in jars of indigo, cochineal, tree bark and wildflowers, we also sold the thread natural and word got around about the thread we made and we started selling to other families, all families from the church. I don't know what Paloma was doing back then, Paloma who was still Gaspar, but she was there like the bushes are there, in the background. And if I say to you that I saw Paloma at the market back then, when I went with my grandfather Cosme, well, I don't remember that exact time but I know she was there and she was still dressing like a boy, and my grandfather said to me, he said, That boy walks like he has feathers. He was the one who first called Paloma "Pájaro", he called her a bird back when she was still Gaspar, and anyone who didn't like Muxes would follow her around calling her "Pájaro".

We dressed in cotton, my grandmother Paz made us light clothes for the hot weather and woollen clothes for the cold, my mother embroidered our clothes with many threads. As we grew, my sister Francisca and I did more work, but our clothes never changed. We mended them, but they never changed. In our town, children dress the same as adults because they start to work as soon as they can walk, like cows are born on their feet, children are born on their feet also to work the land. I see the children who are brought here, the ones who come with the foreigners, and I see how they're given toys to play with and little gadgets.

With the silk we sold to the landowners who lived on estates around San Felipe, my grandfather Cosme and I were able to buy some lambs and some chickens and he sent me and my sister to take care of the animals on the hillside between San Juan de los Lagos and San Felipe, that same place where I went walking with my father before he died, before the fire told that his breath would squeeze tight like the black birds in the sky squeezed tight like a fist to say he had no days or nights left, that fist of black birds that squeezed and then scattered in the dark blue sky to tell my father Felisberto his breath was going to squeeze his life, it was on that hillside there, that's the one, over there by the mountain they'll celebrate next Sunday, these pink candles are for the celebration. For me, that hillside between San Juan de los Lagos and San Felipe is my father, that hillside is where the mushrooms grow that showed me the Language and showed me that I can see the Language in the deep waters because that is God's will. We tended the animals on that hillside and my grandfather Cosme also sent us for the sticks to put the silkworms on, sticks that were round and thin, and he also sent us for dry branches for the kitchen fire that my grandmother Paz made. Francisca and I raised the lambs we bought with the money from the silk until they were big enough that we could sell them and buy others, and that is how we were able to have a small flock.

My sister Francisca and I did all this work as little girls, we didn't play with toys the way children do today. I want to hear what it was like for you and your sister Leandra, but for me, one day I made a rag doll out of the scraps of cotton and wool my grandmother Paz would leave when she sewed, and Francisca made it a little shawl from the scraps of silk my grandmother Paz would dye to sell to the landowners, we named the rag doll María and we played with her. One afternoon, we were talking to her like she was a relative of ours, or a friend, another little girl like me and Francisca, and my grandfather saw us talking to her and scolded us, he told us that no one in our family ever had time to play before, and he tore off the shawl Francisca had made for María with silk clippings and he said to us, Everyone in this house works, my grandfather said, Francisca, Feliciana, idlers are like the dead, those devils bring suffering and they don't even know it, so you two are going to get to work and I don't want any more Tola this, Tola that. But we hadn't named the doll Tola, we'd named her María, and my grandfather never forgot a name, he looked people in the eye and people respected him for that, and no matter what he was doing, he always knew what they had talked about the last time they'd seen each other and he would mention it to people when he saw them at the market, because of that they respected him, and this was the only time I heard him change a name to hurt us, because hurting someone is what forgetting does.

Children in our town do what they like until they can walk, but as soon as they can stand on their own like little cows, it's time for them to work. I remember how my sister Francisca and I had a game where we would put straw on the back of a dog that used to hang around the tilled lands, we'd put a little clump of hay on the back of the dog we'd see around there if it came close to us and it would keep walking with that clump of hay on its back, around and around with that hay until it fell or the wind blew it off its back, and that was the game, to see how long the hay would stay on its back, and we'd both laugh and laugh, but my grandfather Cosme didn't like it when Francisca and I played. My grandfather said Feliciana, Francisca, we treat you the same as we treat everyone in this house, around here we all work to put food on the table and if you learn one thing from me, it'll be respect for work. And he took away the rag doll we named María and he called Tola, which was the name of a woman he hated, and he threw the silk shawl Francisca made into the fire and the flame burnt a bright green I felt in my belly because I saw my sister's face, but he kept the doll that we had named María and he called Tola and later he said, Feliciana you made this doll. My grandfather Cosme kept it for a long time, he never threw it away, and later I understood why.

He took the doll out again, after time had passed. One day, my grandmother Paz fell sick, and that was when I saw Paloma again, who was still Gaspar then. On my father's side of the family all the men were curanderos, so my mother went looking for my father's youngest cousin, Gaspar, who was just a little boy still, barely more than a foal, but he was the only one left from the family of curanderos in our town and all the ones around it. That was how Gaspar started with the Language. Later, Gaspar was Muxe and was Paloma, but back then Gaspar was a curandero and people went to see him because the men of our family had a good reputation. Gaspar was taught by my grandfather and was a helper to my father, he was judged harshly by my grandfather, who called him Pájaro when he was a little boy because he said that Gaspar walked like he had feathers. That was what my grandfather called Muxes who didn't dress like Muxes, he said that men who went with men at night walked like they had feathers. And some people never stopped calling her Pájaro, even though she would say, My name is Paloma, dear, like a dove, because I do love little birds. One time I asked Gaspar why they called him Pájaro and he said Feliciana, some men like to gather with men in the plaza and Pájaros like boys, even though they are boys themselves. Gaspar told me that Muxes were barren like the barren land on the other side of the hill, land where nothing ever grew no matter how much it was burned and tilled, no matter how much rain fell there, because the land was cursed and that was the same reason Muxes had no children. Fine with me, said my grandfather Cosme when he talked about Muxes, we don't need any more like them. When much time had passed, I saw in my ceremonies that there were also women who went with women at night, and once a Muxe came to see me who had the body of a woman, and I saw that Pájaros, which is what my grandfather called them, love just like everyone loves, that they have affections just like everyone does, but my grandfather Cosme was no curandero and he grew up believing that Muxes were horses of a different colour. In my ceremonies, I saw that people love, they fall in love, they have their affections and they suffer and it doesn't matter if they are men or women, and this is something the Language reveals in the ceremonies, we are all the same when it comes to our affections, we are all the same at night, and like they say in the church, we're all the same under the sun, we're all alike under the Language, the Language makes us all equal.

People said that Gaspar liked boys because of a hex someone put on his mother when she was carrying him inside, they said it was a curse for his mother to bring a son into the world who liked boys with big dark eyes like his, who liked eyes as black as night and who liked nights with men, he was her only son and they said that God had punished her for only having one son and not many, like her sister.

The first time I saw Gaspar, when Gaspar was a boy, his face was as beautiful as it always was, with his boyish soft skin and in that first ceremony where I saw him I noticed that he didn't have hair where his arms met his body, or on his legs or anywhere, his voice was just as soft as his skin and he had a scar through his left eyebrow, like from a bad fall. I hadn't had my first moon yet when my mother brought Gaspar to the house carrying something wrapped in banana leaves, carrying it as carefully as how other people carry coins. My first moon came a few days later, I remember thinking that watching the ceremony was what carried me over to the side of women, and I left my sister Francisca behind.

Gaspar brought things to heal my grandmother Paz, whose eyes had sunk into the dark circles around them, and whose skin was white as lime. When he was about to open the banana leaf I looked and saw that there was another wrapping inside of cotton, which I didn't get to see because Gaspar saw that I was looking and scolded me. He was angry, but even so he spoke soft like a stone from the river is soft to the touch from all the water that passes over it and that's how he said to me that he wasn't going to be able to heal my grandmother Paz if I looked at what he had in there, so I stepped back, but I was curious and from a distance I watched them with my eyes almost closed so that if anyone came near they would think I was sleeping and if they were far away they would think I was sleeping and so I was able to see a little bit of what Gaspar did in our house with what he'd wrapped in banana leaves and cotton, he lit a few candles of pure beeswax and he gave what he'd wrapped in banana leaves and cotton to my grandmother Paz, who was very sick. Gaspar bared his chest, he had a beautiful body and delicate movements like I'd never seen before, not in my house or in the market had I ever seen someone move the way Gaspar did, not my grandmother Paz and not my mother, either, they worked the land, they made cloth, and they never touched healthy bodies or sick ones that way, with what seemed to be heat or softness or tenderness or all those things together, and that was how Gaspar touched those banana leaves and those sheets of cotton and then prepared what was inside what I under-stood later were mushrooms, and then he began to sing. His voice was the voice of a boy but the singing softened it, or he softened it before he sang, and with his beautiful face it seemed like he was offering something he'd taken very good care of, the same way you care for the first buds of the spring, that was how Gaspar was caring for the words of the Language. I didn't understand what he was saying, but his words had a melody, his voice was like a corner you like to spend time on, like when the sun is strong in the afternoon and one corner has shade and offers itself and its cool air. A long time passed before I under-stood that what Gaspar did that night was a ceremony and what he took out of the banana-leaf wrappings were the mushrooms he brought to heal my grandmother Paz, the kind of mushrooms I'd seen with my father Felisberto, who never told me what they were used for, he only told me how to tell certain ones from the others and my father said, this is the Book, Feliciana, and it is yours, and I didn't understand what he meant. I had seen those mushrooms before, on the hillside between San Juan de los Lagos and San Felipe, where Francisca and I tended our sheep.

The night of the ceremony to heal my grandmother, I closed my eyes and pretended to be asleep, and I tried to understand what Gaspar was singing. I understood certain words, he was singing about the stars, with his soft voice he sang about clouds, about the force of air, of the whirlwind, of two whirlwinds that come together to form one strong one, and about winds that fall tame, about white stars in the black night, and he said to my grand-mother, he said, You are the white star in the black night. He said, I am man, I am woman, I am priest and priestess, I am the white star in the black night that comes to bring light to the shadows. That was the first time I travelled, I left the house where we lived, and with that beautiful voice of his, his voice was so beautiful, he made the Language beautiful. That was the first time I was free, when Gaspar the young boy chanted I was free, in that moment I could do what I wanted because of his beautiful voice. The more you heard his voice, the more you wanted to take shelter inside it, the way he used the Language gave shelter, my sister Francisca was deep in her dreams but I didn't want to miss what came at the end of Gaspar's song. Around dawn, but before the sun came out of its mountain, Gaspar took something that looked like dirt and some white powder that came from the entrails of an animal he carried over one shoulder, and he rubbed them on my grandmother's chest, and also on my mother's chest and on my grandfather Cosme, even though they hadn't eaten the mushrooms, and then he smeared the dirt and the powder on his own chest. When sun began to rise, my grandmother also rose and now she didn't look weak. Gaspar gave her life. Everyone knows that when a person is very sick, it seems like a gasp could send them to the burial place, or that death could come on a heavy wind to lay its egg in them. That first gasp brought my grandmother Paz back, she grew stronger that night with the things Gaspar gave her to eat and smeared on her body, for days she couldn't stand, until Gaspar stroked her gently with his voice and the Language, until he told her that her ceremony had ended and that she was going to feel better. And she did.

A few days after the ceremony when I had my first moon, I was tending the sheep and the goats on the hillside with Francisca, we were sitting under a tree and I saw mushrooms all around us, just like the ones my father

Felisberto showed me before he died. My grandparents Cosme and Paz spoke about the mushrooms with respect in their voices, even though none of their ancestors had been curanderos. My mother spoke with respect about the curanderos in my father's family, she had known them and knew about the things they did, knew that they were loved by many people. My grandmother Paz recovered from her sickness after the ceremony with Gaspar, and that was how I learned that the mushrooms were good and I thought maybe I could try them. That was when I found out that my grandfather Cosme had kept the doll I made named María that he called Tola, because it was there with the things he placed around my grandmother Paz, and Gaspar saw my grandfather Cosme holding the doll I named María and he said to him, That girl is of the Book. And I didn't understand what he was saying.

I was ten or thirteen years old, a few days after I had my first moon, when I tried a mushroom for the first time with my sister Francisca, who was a little girl for a while longer, but not very long. We tried it under the shade tree, one afternoon when we were tending our sheep and our goats. That time, I remember the mushrooms took away our hunger and cheered our afternoon. Sometimes, when my sister Francisca and I were hungry and there wasn't enough food for the five of us in the house where we lived, we'd take the sheep and the goats to the hillside and share a mushroom, and that would tame our hunger.

One time, my grandfather Cosme showed up at the shade tree where my sister Francisca and I were sitting, watching the sheep and the goats and he found us there laughing, laughing like we couldn't stop and we couldn't, it was a festivity and since my grandfather Cosme didn't like laughing he said to us, Enjoy this smile on my face because I only smile when snow falls on our town, but snow never fell on San Felipe, only hail and sorrows, so while we were loose with laughing we also worried that he was going to be angry, that he was going to be furious, but nothing could stop our laughing, like when you drop a stone and nothing can stop it from falling and if he yelled at us it was only going to make us laugh more because our laughter fell like a stone, and I thought my grandfather Cosme was going to get angry and I went soft thinking he might get angry and I think he understood that and he started laughing at how my sister Francisca and I were laughing and he also understood that my sister Francisca and I had eaten a mushroom and he didn't yell, instead he carried us home and didn't say a word about it to my mother or my grandmother Paz.

During the next rains I went back to the hillside between San Juan de los Lagos and San Felipe with my sister Francisca and we ate mushrooms again, this time one for her and one for me. My sister Francisca had also had her moon during the rains and I remember her saying to me, Feliciana, I had my first moon, and that was the first time I had a vision that I remember clearly, there was a strong wind and the leaves and the branches were moving in the wind and in between them I saw the face of my father Felisberto that had been with me since I could speak. I felt his love, he was there with me, alive. He looked at me, he was dressed well and it made me happy to see him dressed that way, looking happy and healthy, he told me that my sister Francisca and I were well cared for, that I should pray to God and say thank you because I should be grateful for all that was coming to me, he asked me to thank God always because many big things awaited me. And he told me to take care of my sister Francisca because she would always be with me, at my side, and I promised him I would, and he said to me, Feliciana, the Book is yours. I don't know how to write, no one in my family does, so that seemed strange, and this thing he said to me in my vision was the same thing he'd said to me in life, and was the same thing I heard Gaspar say to my grandfather Cosme, before he was Paloma, Gaspar said, That girl holds the Language, the Book is hers. I didn't understand yet.

When I came back from the vision, I told my sister Francisca that I had seen my father Felisberto and I told her the things he said to me, and she asked me what he looked like and I told her that we both looked more like him than like our mother, her even more than me. That made her happy. I knew I was on the path because I felt it to be so, I felt it clearly but I didn't know where to go next, my father Felisberto was the first person to tell me about the path that I sensed was mine but I didn't know how to follow it when I was just a girl but when Paloma was still Gaspar he came to me and said, Feliciana, come visit me one day and I'll show you how to find the Language and the Book so you can understand that it's yours, and I said, The Bible? and he said, No, Feliciana.

In the vision I had, my father Felisberto said something to me to prove he wasn't a spirit and that I wasn't imagining him, he told me to tell my grandfather Cosme that I was going to follow my father and his father and his father who were curanderos, and my father said that my grandfather Cosme was going to cross his arms and say that this path is only for men to travel. But if a flower is born a flower there's no way to make it a bush, no matter how much someone might want it to be a bush, and that is what I came here to tell you, Feliciana, he said, this is what you are going to answer him, and with this answer you are going to prove to your grandfather Cosme that this is your path, you will prove it to everyone, because you are not going to say, This is my path because it was the path of my father Felisberto and my grandfather and my great-grandfather, you are going to say, This path is mine because I am Feliciana.

And that was how I learned my path and saw the path in my own name. I saw it and felt it when I was still a girl. I don't speak Spanish or English or German or French or any of the tongues that the people who come to see me speak, I can't speak to them in their tongues, I've been in films and in newspapers, they send me books, records, the things the artists make they send me, and I always tell them, Thank you, but I don't care if I'm the first or the last or if they talk about me, I don't care but thank you, I do what I do because this is my path and if I've been in films and newspapers and books and photographs it's because that is what appeared along the path with my name, but I don't seek that out, those people who come to speak with me in other tongues, I can only answer in my tongue, and I won't kill my tongue with another, I don't speak the government's tongue, which is why they have to bring their interpreters so they can tell the people what I say, just as what I say to you now reaches you in another tongue, it doesn't reach you in mine. This seems fine to me, because even when two people try to understand each other in the same tongue they can't, one person understands one thing and the other person understands something else, and this is why the Language is as broad and vast as the present. After my father spoke to me, a long time after, when I already had my three children Aniceta, Apolonia, and Aparicio, and when I was already Nicanor's widow, I stepped onto my path to heal the afflictions in people's bodies and in their souls, and I told my grandfather Cosme, This is my path, God's path is my own, the path of healing and of helping people look into their deep waters is mine. And my grandfather Cosme crossed his arms and told me that the path was only for men to travel, just as my father had said, and I knew I would have to prove my path to my grandfather Cosme, just as my father had said. I had to prove it to him and to everyone, which is what my father had meant when he said Feliciana, you are a woman on the path of men and you have been given something they never were given, not because they are men but because you are you, and that something was the Book my father Felisberto told me about before he died, the Book Paloma said belonged to the girl I was, but the Book still had not appeared before me.

8

My mother left home when she was sixteen. She got along well with her siblings, but her relationship with her parents was tense. She wanted to live on her own terms. The situation got complicated when, as a teenager, she realised that the only way she could pursue her dream of getting a degree and a job was by moving out. My grandparents had six children, two of them girls: my mother and my aunt, who's six years younger. At sixteen, my mother was already being pressured by my grandparents to get married, mostly because their understanding of the world didn't include the possibility that a woman might go to college or get a job; the only way she was going to be able to do either of those things was without their consent. They disapproved vehemently at first, but they began to soften their position when she moved out – after my grandmother had already guilted her mercilessly, of course. My mother's decision to leave home shaped the way she saw the world and, later, the way she raised me and Leandra. She worked at a clothing store during her university years – one time she pointed out a parking lot where the shop used to be – and she went everywhere on her bicycle. Her salary paid for a room in a house where she lived with other students, including my uncle, my father's brother. That's how they met.

Over those months we spent with our grandparents, Leandra ate compulsively and lost all interest in school – killing time in her classes, doodling in her notebooks, warming her seat. She stayed afloat in the first school that kicked her out because she was smart and knew how to get by. That school expelled her because she kept getting marked down for her attitude; later, after she turned eleven, she grew way more rebellious than her classmates. Leandra was three years younger than me, which meant that she set the pace in some things. I got my period later than most of my classmates, partly because I'd skipped a grade, and partly because I had synchronised with Leandra in certain ways. She was one of the first in her cohort to get hers.

My maternal grandmother was a devout Catholic and we went to church with her while we lived in their house. She was ashamed of Leandra's rebellious streak, and often made remarks about her short hair, sometimes calling her a tomboy – that was the term she used – and my sister would tell her that there were other ways of dressing, other hairstyles, than the ones she knew about. Leandra didn't care about school, she didn't care about studying, and between her charisma and her sense of humour she could spin a whole classroom out of control. If anything ever happened at the school, if anything ever went wrong, Leandra was always one of the suspects. To the surprise of our whole family, including my aunt, who was always close to and protective of my sister, Leandra suddenly developed an interest in the priest's sermons when our grandmother dragged us with her to church; before bed, she'd pray on her knees with her hands clasped and her eyes closed, and one day, out of nowhere, she told me that she wanted to take Holy Communion. I don't know how, but a few minutes later she'd convinced me to sign up for Sunday School with her at the church near my grand-parents' house, where my father would grudgingly drop us off every weekend once the four of us were living together again. Leandra was ten, almost eleven, when we made our first Holy Communion; I was thirteen and felt like a bear on a unicycle.

Our first Holy Communion was a group affair. All the families involved organised a party and my aunt, who was gentle and understanding with Leandra, gave her a Zippo Spectrum they'd seen at the mall one time they'd gone to see a film. My sister thought it was the coolest thing on Earth. The idea was my aunt's boyfriend's – they'd agreed that it was the perfect gift to accompany the Catholic cross, the sheaf of wheat tied with a bone-coloured ribbon, and the large candle she was supposed to light every night while she prayed. Leandra had begged my aunt's boyfriend to give her his silver Zippo, which she'd thought was the greatest invention ever. She boasted that the flame wouldn't go out: she tested it with her hand and tried to blow it out, it blew her mind that it resisted even the wind coming in through the window between our beds, and that night, when we opened the few gifts we'd received, most of which were inspired by our grandmother's religious zeal, Leandra lit her candle for the first time with her Zippo Spectrum. The same lighter she'd use not long after to start a fire in the third school she was kicked out of.

As if our mother was a lost cause and she finally had a chance to share her faith with her eldest grandchildren, my grandmother gave us each a white dress and a Bible bound in mother-of-pearl plastic with our names written in an ecclesiastical font inside, which made us seem like saints, and sterling silver medals of Christ that neither of us were ever going to wear. She told us our uncles had given us a photo album that she'd bought, with the words MY FIRST COMMUNION embossed on the cover in gold, and the gilded silhouettes of two children praying face to face. In accordance with his atheism, my father didn't participate in the religious ceremony, he stood through the whole thing, refusing to kneel when the priest called for it, refusing to respond or to pray with the rest of us. He liked to joke that if he had more free time, he'd go door to door spreading the Good Word of atheism, and that pretty much summed up our religious sensibility at home.

Leandra was thrilled with her Zippo. She lit it and put it out, flipped it open and shut, and that night I began to leaf through the book of poems my aunt gave me. My gift is better than yours because mine can burn yours, said Leandra from her bed, while I tried to decide if I wanted to read the book or not – it seemed pretty serious, words were more imposing organised vertically than they were in the seventies magazines I was used to. That night, though, I decided to give it a chance before going to sleep. I'll never forget what that book did to me at the age of thirteen, it was as if I'd studied the catechism and made my first Communion for the sole purpose of understanding that line by Fernando Pessoa: "If God is not One, how can I be?"

I discovered everything that summer. As if someone had forgotten to mention that the thing I'd been doing for thirteen years – living – could also be fun. That book was my gateway to film, music, newspapers; to questioning my parents. That summer I got my period for the first time, and even though the physical changes and emotional rollercoaster frightened me at first, like someone had thrown me into a pool to teach me how to swim, I was happy to feel it put some distance between me and Leandra, at least for a while.

I started writing bad poetry. Terrible poetry. I started

writing articles for the school paper, which was just xeroxes of adolescent tantrums stapled together, and decided I wanted to learn to play an instrument. I liked the drums. I asked my father for lessons. My father was an engineer and didn't know a thing about music or, I suspect, about dealing with a teenage daughter who was beginning to express herself. If anyone celebrated the things I wrote it was him, but he didn't know what to do with my interest in the drums and said I should ask my mother. She told me to find drum lessons close to home that weren't too expensive.

I found a guy who was just under thirty with long hair and a t-shirt with the cover of Nirvana's *Nevermind* printed on it, who lived with his parents in a house made almost entirely of wood and adobe that smelled like a cabin in the woods. Its rural vibe seemed odd to me, there in the middle of the city: it had wooden decorations and a cowhide rug under their rustic dining table, clay pots in different sizes as accents, and a giant bone-coloured macramé hanging on the wall. He tried to come across like a bad boy in the way he dressed and talked; he told me, as he sipped the lemonade his mother had probably made for him, that he'd only taught guys, that I was the first girl to show up looking for lessons. If you think about it, he said, halfway through his lemonade, there aren't any female drummers. No woman has ever made rock history. Yeah, he said, finishing his drink in a single gulp, women sing, they don't play instruments – and definitely not the drums.

It was a Saturday afternoon, and Leandra was leaving the house with her backpack slung over her shoulder. I asked her where she was headed, and she replied, No, Zoe, I'm not going to set a fire in the park. Then she slammed the door. Leandra had just turned eleven and had been kicked out of school for the first time because a few of the teachers had gotten together and agreed that her behaviour was a problem, despite her intelligence and the good grades she got thanks to her excellent memory. Leandra got bored in class and preferred hanging out with her peers; she made friends easily, but she was a distraction. The final straw was when she challenged a teacher who had the power to decide whether she passed the grade or not. She pushed the envelope so far that the teacher finally lost patience, and even though she performed amazingly on the test, getting the highest score of the whole cohort, he called a faculty meeting to discuss Leandra's case, which already included a long list of complaints against her. They decided to pass her, but she had to switch schools. That's how she ended up at the second school that expelled her.

That school was in an old building that had a ceiling fan in every room. When the teacher would turn her back, someone would toss a pencil sharpener or an eraser at the fan, which would make a noise just loud enough to get everyone laughing. When the teacher wasn't there and the fan was on, they'd toss pencils and pens up there – once, someone threw their whole pencil case – and the objects would go flying across the room, to everyone's delight. One day, when the teacher stepped out to talk to another faculty member, Leandra soaked a jacket with a bottle of water and tossed it up at the fan. The whole thing came down and brought with it a good chunk of the ceiling, leaving a large hole that Leandra called "the crater". That, together with other citations for bad conduct, was enough to get her kicked out again.

The day she passed me on her way to the park, she was wearing a black zip-up sweatshirt. She'd often get together with a friend of hers who lived in one of the buildings facing the park. He almost always wore a rasta beanie and had a round nose and big eyes; he was sweet and had a soft spot for my sister. I made the most of having our room to myself that afternoon and put on a song I knew by heart to try out my singing voice, when my mother came in and asked what had happened to my drum lessons. I had gotten home early and my father wasn't there, and it made me uncomfortable that she'd come in without knocking. I told her what the instructor had said. She sat her thirty-something self down on the corner of my bed – with her red lipstick and her hair falling loose, a gold chain accenting her white t-shirt, and her high-waisted jeans – and said,

What a monumental idiot, Zoe, with those stereotypes about women. Please. You know what you should have said to him, you should have said that no mind as small as his has made rock history, and then slammed the door in his face. You're not telling me that bonehead killed your interest in playing the drums, are you?

I found another instructor willing to teach a group of eight teenagers the basics of drums, guitar, and piano. He was in his twenties and had red hair and eyelashes, pale skin, and freckles sprinkled across his face like ground cinnamon. He was really tall and always had his eyes half-closed, and his body seemed too big for him to move it with any precision. We all adored him. The classes were held in the back of his father's house. His father was a respected psychoanalyst who popped his head in every now and then to say hello; one time we saw television cameras set up in the garden between the house and the studio – a celebrity had killed herself and he was being interviewed about his writings on suicide. He was a big name, and had recently moved his office to a building in another neighbourhood, which he shared with other psychoanalysts, psychologists and therapists. Our instructor was getting his Master's in classical guitar and taught our lessons in the afternoon to cover his expenses. He was fun and kind to us, he gave us confidence.

I met María in those music classes. She was into the

guitar, and together we formed a band called Neon. In the margins of her notebooks, she'd invented a character called Neon Girl whose superpower was that she could glow – I'm not sure under what circumstances, or what the point of that would even be – but we liked the idea that she stood out for being neon. We started practising on Saturday afternoons, sometimes under the name Neon, and sometimes Neon Girl, until we decided that our "official" name would be Neon. Then Julia joined; she was María's neighbour and had a good voice. She was more lively and extroverted in our rehearsals than she was the few times we played in public. Julia felt uncomfortable in front of people, but she sang well. Still, her energy in rehearsal was the polar opposite of how she was on stage, she was like two different people: the few times we played for a small audience, she covered part of her face with her bangs and sang with her eyes closed or glued to the floor.

We played our first show outdoors, frightened to death, in a battle of the bands organised by the district where María and Julia lived as part of a youth talent festival. Our families went, plus a couple of people who just wandered in; our music instructor brought his girlfriend and congratulated us effusively when we went to say hello, and even gave us a bouquet of yellow flowers. We came in second, which, according to Leandra, who was there with her backpack and her rasta-beanie-wearing friend, was the worst possible ranking: we weren't in first place, but we weren't hidden away in the pit of third place, either, where everyone would just forget about us. We were stuck with the tepid, miserly accolade of second place in a local competition.

We also played the birthday party of one of the kids in our music lessons. We did better that time, and we had more fun. After that, we played at the year-end party at the school I went to, the first one to kick Leandra out; the students put on a kind of talent show. I remember Leandra showing up alone that time, in a kimono open over blue pants, a white tank top, and black boots. She met up with some friends, and one girl gave her an enthusiastic hug before sitting down next to her. Her friend cheered for each of the performances; Leandra didn't clap or show interest in a single one other than ours. We were up after a boy who recited love poems from memory. We were ready to go on stage and I remember seeing Leandra with a hand to her forehead as if she couldn't stand one more verse out of that boy, so theatrically bored in her kimono. She'd recently started getting her period and was losing weight; she liked to joke that she was on a pasta diet, which was true. Not only had her metabolism changed, she wasn't eating compulsively anymore.

We played a couple of covers of bands we listened to back then, which were well received, and then a few songs we'd written ourselves. María composed the melodies and I wrote the lyrics. In those days, Leandra was a secret smoker: my paternal grandfather had died with grey skin from emphysema, and tobacco was like kryptonite to our father. He could down a whole bottle of whiskey or tequila, but he hated cigarettes, he couldn't stand the smell and it would have upset him to know that Leandra smoked. My sister, who liked to push the envelope, didn't want to hurt my father, but she didn't want to quit smoking, either, so she went outside to smoke with her friend after we finished our set. My parents were in the audience and I remember watching Leandra walk right up to us; reeking of mint chewing gum and sipping coffee from a styrofoam cup, she told us confidently that she liked the songs we'd written but that they were like triplets, it was hard to tell them apart. And she was right. I wrote other lyrics, looking up synonyms in the dictionary to make them more interesting. When I showed them to Leandra, though, she told me that she didn't understand the lyrics but the songs were okay, that I'd done some *serious anthropological work* there, digging around in the rubble for complicated words. Her comment hit home; it stayed with me because I trusted Leandra, and only Leandra, to be honest.

I used to practise in the garage, listening to albums from start to finish; sometimes during practice my father would dance, a little stiffly, when he heard something he liked. The first time we met at María's house to practise after Leandra's comment, I suggested we try a rap. We wrote it between the three of us, sticking mostly to the rhythm of the drums and a sample from Tupac. Leandra didn't like that song, either, but we performed it at a party at Julia's house. Julia sang with her hair in front of her face, a purple cap on her head, and neon yellow nail polish. In the middle of the song, María improvised something about the party, and that was a big hit.

When we were fourteen or fifteen, we traded the band and the neon nails for parties, and soon Neon felt like ancient history. It even embarrassed me a little when someone would mention one of our songs, but I kept writing music after the band broke up, songs I never sang or played in public – and never showed to Leandra, whose judgement could be pretty intimidating – but the drum set I bought at a market stall with used instruments let me put a beat to the poems I wrote. Sometimes on the weekend, while my father took apart his or some co-worker's car and put it back together, I'd spend the afternoon playing the drums, singing words to a beat that made them sound better, the same way I couldn't just eat a spoonful of sugar unless it was dissolved in a cup of coffee. Maybe I got that from my dad, the need to dissolve one thing into another.

I didn't stop reading or writing articles for the school paper. Leandra never cared much about books or periodicals. When we were teenagers, it seemed like we would just keep growing like the two parallel lines of our beds under the window in the bedroom we shared, that our paths would never meet and after we left home we wouldn't have much of a relationship, except for maybe running into one another at family gatherings.

Leandra went through a radical change over the course of just a few months. All of a sudden, she wasn't an overweight pre-teen with dimpled hands and short hair; all of a sudden, she was a good-looking teenager. She liked to play with that. The first time she got drunk, she outdrank all her friends. They were at a party and the beer and vodka had run out. Leandra had been the only one who mixed the liqueurs that belonged to the parents of the girl who'd invited everyone over. My father had needed to go pick her up that night; he'd carried her into the house and as he tucked her in, he'd sent me to the kitchen for a plastic bucket to put between our beds.

Leandra spent more and more time away from home, we barely ran into each other. I went to parties where we smoked joints, drank canned lager, and had conversations we thought were going to change the world; Leandra, on the other hand, went to all sorts of parties. I wore Converse, Leandra wore boots. You'll never catch me in Converse, Zoe, she once said, they're part of the heinous uniform of capitalism.

Back then, the seniors at one of the high schools would

hold these big afternoon parties, where everyone would get together to eat, drink, and hook up. The lucky ones ended up making out or fucking in a corner. These parties – which started around three, when the morning students got out of school, and ended in late-night melodrama – were so popular that every now and then a good band would show up to play them. The only time I went to one was to see a local band that María and I really liked. We met a couple there, two boys; we got along great with them and passed joints back and forth in the grass until night fell. That was the only party I saw Leandra at in all that time. She was drunk and asked me not to point out how drunk she was, then, with her nose all red she said to me, I'd like you to meet my wife, Zoe – she's my friend's girlfriend but I thought she was so cool I asked her to marry me and we did . . . get married . . . but don't tell mum and dad I got married and didn't invite them to the wedding. My voice was a little deeper than hers back then, not much more, but I noticed that Leandra was speaking in a higher pitch than usual, and found it strange; I associated it, I don't know why, with her wanting to impress the girl, who wore a sweet perfume and had a sweet voice. The next morning, she told me that they'd kissed and it had been a lot of fun.

Leandra wanted to be a designer, which my father found unsettling. Maybe because it was the opposite of his practical work as an engineer. My mother usually neutralised those conversations. I wanted to write for a newspaper, do research in a library or maybe write poetry, which put me on a frequency my parents just couldn't pick up. I remember telling them once that one day I was going to write all kinds of articles for the paper where I worked and it was like I'd just planted a flag on the moon, the concept was so foreign to my family. When I told Feliciana how I'd ended up at my job, she'd said with total confidence that I had the Language, too, but that something was still missing. I guess the Language was a pretty foreign concept for me, at first – it seemed like something magical, totally esoteric. Little by little, though, I realised she was talking about something broader.

And what do you plan to do about it? my mother asked me one day. Jobs don't just come knocking on your door, you have to go out and get them. One morning on my way to school I bought the newspaper my father read every Saturday, a habit he'd picked up from my paternal grand-father, who was also an engineer. I suspected it didn't interest him as much as it helped him maintain a relation-ship with his father, just like how having the same job had been a silent way of staying close – if my father was a man of few words, my grandfather was a tomb. It was the same newspaper I sometimes read when I kept him company in the garage, and I looked up the address and stopped by their offices that same afternoon to offer my services. It was a big company so I thought they might have a job for me, and besides, it was the paper my father bought, the one that showed up on our doorstep every morning like a faithful dog. I had no idea how anything worked, but I think I was so determined that I managed to get the receptionist to put me in touch with the assistant of the man who edited the culture section, and he asked me to come back on Monday. It wasn't easy to reach the Editor in Chief, but when I finally did, he told me there weren't any openings for little girls with too much time on their hands. We work here, he said, this isn't a place you come to kill time. I didn't get past the waiting room. When I told my parents about it, they were in the kitchen eating sandwiches in front of the television with the volume down. My father stayed calm; he told me I should go back and try to get the gentleman to listen to me. My mother exploded.

"Who told that clown you were a little girl looking to kill time? I don't know where Lord Editor got his manners, but if you don't put him in his place, I will. Your father's right. You're going back there, and you're not just going to put him in his place, you're going to show him that you're qualified for that or any other job you want, Zoe."

The next day, at a time when she should have been at work, my mother was there waiting for me when I got out of school to drive me to the newspaper offices.

"The pay's going to be awful, but they should have

something for you. I'll wait here until you come back with a job. And don't even think about working for free, it's never the right thing to do, ever. No matter how new you are to something."

We had to go back the following week because the editor wasn't in, but his assistant promised I'd be seen again. I had school in the mornings, so I was given the afternoon shift and Saturdays from 7:00am to noon, along with a shitty salary.

I learned pretty quickly that there was no such thing as a good shift in a newsroom; I ended up having to go in all weekend, but I earned the respect of my first boss there, who recommended me for my first job after school, and that job brought me to my current one. The afternoon I was hired was one of those predictably schizoid summer days – intense heat in the morning, followed by a downpour that started like clockwork in the early evening – and I remember my mother behind the wheel in a black sweater and orange lipstick, with her nails painted red.

"The problem with fleas is bigger than it seems, Zoe. If you put a whole bunch of fleas in a glass jar they'll jump and hit the lid, because, well, fleas jump. But did you know that if you take the lid off, they still only jump as far as that invisible limit because they can't imagine the lid isn't there anymore? The same thing happens in a sexist system. Neither of you have that problem, not you or your sister, never forget that you can both jump as high as you want. If the jar has a lid, it's up to you to take it off."

I worked at that newspaper for five years, and in all that time my mother never stopped calling my boss Lord Editor. She never forgave him for that first encounter. Out of all the applications to the Communications course the year I applied, eighty students were admitted and only ten received financial support. It was a major accomplishment for me to get one of those fellowships, not only because it was exactly what I wanted to do, but also because I'd worked my arse off for six months to get in; I studied maths, chemistry and physics after school, finding time where I could at the paper. When the results were announced, my father called me from the office to say he was so proud of me and that he was going to do something special to celebrate. At the time I thought he was talking about a dinner, but it was the '78 Valiant. When I saw my mother at home, she tossed out an "I expected no less of you," and that day I finally understood. It was her way of saying that doing what I wanted was exactly what she expected of me.

9

My grandfather Cosme didn't talk to me again after I told him that this was my path, that the path of God is mine. I healed the people who came to see me and they began to talk about how I healed them, more and more people came when word began to spread that I healed illnesses of the body and the soul and they began to come from the next towns over and people who spoke Spanish began to come, and then people came who spoke other tongues, foreigners began to come to San Felipe asking for me, they came on horseback and on mules, they cut paths with machetes to come, the foreigners came however they could, with people from town as their guides. Back then there were no highways or even paved roads, the mayor put those in when he saw all the foreigners coming, he wanted to make a good impression on the foreigners, the mayor heard that a gringo banker came because he saw the film they made about me and he said that's a powerful man and he even invited the banker to his house. Back then, to get to my house by the milpas you had to travel four or five hours on horseback or mule, and on foot sometimes, and cut your way through with a machete if branches had come down with the last hailstorm, and even so people came, so many came that I had to say to them, Come back tomorrow, my child, come back another day, and you, come back later, but of all the people who came to see me, the one I most wanted to hear say that what I was doing was good was my grandfather Cosme, he was the one who told me I was doing men's work.

One day, my grandfather Cosme showed up at my door and he said, Feliciana, I hear you're a famous curandera, I hear that you have the Language and I've come to give you my blessing. That's how he was, he was slow to say things but then when he did say them, his door was wide open and it was a very big door. My grandfather Cosme opened his door to me just two times and that was the second, the first was when I married Nicanor. I was around fourteen when I married Nicanor, I don't know the exact number, they don't make papers when people are born here in San Felipe or in San Juan de los Lagos. When I had my first daughter, Aniceta, that was when my grandfather opened his door to me the first time, because he held his spites in until they came out. My grandfather Cosme showed up at my door with the rag doll I'd made when I was a little girl, the one I'd named María and he'd called Tola, and he said to me, Feliciana, this belongs to your daughter Aniceta now, but take it from her when she plays so she can find her way, just like I taught you how to work. And I knew that my grandfather Cosme was opening his door to me, when I married Nicanor and had my daughter Aniceta. I knew that he loved me even though he never said it, and that he respected me as a curandera, I knew those things the second time he opened his door to me. My grandfather Cosme never loved Paloma, he spoke to her with words like machetes, people loved Paloma but my grandfather Cosme was hard on her. He never said thank you when Paloma who was still Gaspar raised my grandmother Paz from her sickness because he'd seen the feathers on him, and if he ever heard someone say something about Paloma he'd say that he walked like he had feathers.

Before Nicanor's family, three other families came to see if my grandfather Cosme would give me to them, but the families didn't bring the boys, you weren't allowed to see the boy before the wedding, no, no I never met them, but I met their families. Nicanor's family was the biggest and kindest, they had goats, hens, a few pigs, and my grandfather gave his approval and I met Nicanor later, a few days before our wedding in the town church. I thought he was very serious. He came with a bride price of a few pigs and goats that my grandmother Paz looked after. My grandfather Cosme slaughtered a goat and my mother made atole for everyone, and Nicanor's big family brought liquor and turkey in mole. On the day of the wedding, Nicanor told me that he could read and write because they'd sent him to the community school. Nicanor's family also gave the music at our wedding, the Montes Band was the sound of inns and parties in San Felipe and travelled to other towns in the region, you know the kind with dancers and all and, well, the Montes Band brought music to our wedding because one of them was a relative of Nicanor's and his family was all there. Paloma didn't have men yet, she didn't go with men she loved at night or with men she didn't love, she was still the boy Gaspar, still a curandero, and that night Gaspar danced with all the women in Nicanor's family, and they all liked him, he was good to be around and great at parties, and all the women in Nicanor's family liked him, he got them all to laugh and to dance while my grandfather Cosme went around saying that Gaspar wasn't part of his family, that he was from my father Felisberto's side and what a shame it was that he was the last of the long line of curanderos. At the dance, my sister Francisca came to me and said, Feliciana, I don't want them to marry me off, and she spent the whole wedding silent like an owl, her eyes wide and watching, caring for the children in Nicanor's family, who were many.

I was frightened during the first days of my marriage with Nicanor, partly because I had always slept on the same mat with my sister Francisca, partly because Nicanor liked to eat a big breakfast and we weren't used to that, and partly because I didn't understand what was happening when he climbed onto me on our wedding night. I accepted it, I thought this is the life of a married woman, but I didn't understand why people like to climb onto each other, that was something it took me time to understand in my marriage with Nicanor. I thought, this is the custom between men and women, people like this, I thought, so I should just follow the custom. My sister Francisca asked me what I meant that Nicanor climbed onto me, she was frightened that her own wedding day would arrive and said she didn't want my grandfather Cosme to marry her off, because he was already talking about it, in the plaza he would talk about his granddaughter Francisca with people who already knew her as tall and a beauty. It took me time, but then later I understood why some people climb onto others and enjoy it, it took me time to realise it was nice. Nicanor was a boy then and he didn't drink, but he had to drink the liquor his family brought on our wedding day, we both drank the liquor because they made us, but what we both really liked was working. Back then I didn't know and had no way of knowing that Nicanor would give himself over to alcohol the way he did after being a soldier, he gave himself over to it until they hacked him to death with a machete when my son Aparicio was taking his first steps.

At the beginning of our marriage, I saw that it was nice to be married with Nicanor, I married him before I knew him, I met his family first so we started knowing each other and later we saw that it was nice to be married. When I told him I was pregnant, he was neither happy or sad, it was like I'd told him storms follow mornings that the sun clears, Nicanor said nothing when I told him I was pregnant, it was like I'd told him it was morning and he said to me, Feliciana, make me some sweet coffee like I take it, and that day I told him I was pregnant he took the news like he took the coffee I made him before the sun came out of its mountain.

When I birthed Aniceta my grandfather Cosme came and opened his door to me, and Gaspar came to me also and said, Feliciana, I'm not clean, I can't heal people anymore. And so people started going to One-eyed Tadeo who read kernels of corn and took advantage, telling people what they wanted to hear, he tossed his seven kernels and told the future, he took advantage of people who believed he could see the future because he had one eye, and Gaspar came to tell me that he'd gone at night with a man who had a family, a politician from the city who had children and a wife and who came to work with the mayor, he'd gone to the pulquería somewhere no one he knew would see him to pick up a boy, and there was Gaspar, who was still a boy, and I saw death lay its egg in Gaspar for the first time, before he was Paloma, death laid its egg in Gaspar not because the politician had children and a wife, but because he went from town to town going with boys and he carried a disease that he gave to Gaspar. Gaspar came to see me then and said pus was coming out of him instead of urine, how could he get rid of it, he said, Feliciana, help me with the herbs you bless. We went to the hillside to bless herbs and over time they cured Gaspar's sickness from the time he went with that politician at night. I was carrying Aniceta in my shawl and Gaspar said to me, Feliciana, dear, that little girl and that smile of hers will put everything right. He loved Aniceta ever since she was born, later he got along well with Apolonia but he loved Aniceta, he came to see me because of her, and that's how we came to see each other so much, Gaspar came to our house and worked alongside us. Apolonia was born quickly, and Aparicio was born quickly when I was in my marriage with Nicanor.

In those days, Nicanor went off with revolutionaries to ride horseback and carry a rifle, first they put lead in his arm with a rifle, then in his horse, then they put lead in his belly. He sent me messages through different people and sent me coins so I could take care of things. In those days my grandmother Paz died, and not long after my grandfather Cosme followed her. He couldn't bear the sadness without her, I saw it that day we had a hail storm. My grandfather Cosme died because my grandmother Paz had gone, he was healthy, death laid its egg in his soul, not in his body, because death is like that, my grandfather

Cosme went not long after my grandmother Paz. And not long after that, my mother joined them, too, the three of them went like fire spreads in a hard wind, the three of them went in the rainy season, in one rainy season the three of them were gone. My sister Francisca was relieved that my grandfather Cosme hadn't married her off.

And so there are deaths of companionship, there are people who die so they can follow the one who went before them, then death lays its egg in a person's soul because they ask it to and if it doesn't they try to take its egg the way people snatch things in the market, but death is always there to trill its song. Because death listens to people, just how life listens. My grandfather Cosme stopped talking when my grandmother Paz died, he went mute, his mouth sank in because his words were gone, he didn't want to use his mouth, not even to eat with, it sank in the way your arm falls asleep if you don't use it, my grandfather Cosme stopped talking as if that was his way of leaving the earth and then one day it was morning and his body was cold. I can't say my grandfather Cosme died, he stopped talking because God stopped giving him words, he stopped talking after my grandmother Paz died and then my sister Francisca came to tell me grandpa Cosme was with God. And she looked relieved because she didn't want my grandfather Cosme to marry her off, he had already received one family interested in my sister Francisca, but they didn't have cattle for the bride price, and the other week, after my grandfather died, another family was supposed to go see him with the bride price but then they didn't appear.

My mother had a sickness of the heart that put her out like a candle that burns down in the night while everyone is asleep. Only my sister Francisca and I were left, me and my three children Aniceta, Apolonia and Aparicio, and Nicanor who was with the revolutionaries in their war. Gaspar, who wasn't yet Paloma, came to help us with our work.

In those days, there were soldiers who would go to the houses of other soldiers to leave the coins they made in the army, and soldiers sent spoken messages for their women at home and the children waiting for them there, and the few who could read and write sent letters. Nicanor sent me letters because he knew how to read and write, but I don't know how to read so I would ask the soldier who brought me the letter to read it to me, and then later I'd ask someone else to read it again, and again, just for the pleasure of hearing what Nicanor said to me. He said for me not to worry because all the soldiers were going to come back fine and real soon, but soon after that a soldier knocked on my door to say Nicanor had died in battle. I cried, I took in the idea that Nicanor had died and I worked up the courage to tell my children, We're going to say goodbye to your father Nicanor, we're going to make him an empty grave so we have somewhere to mourn him even if we're only crying to his name because that doesn't die, names don't have hours or times because the name we use when the person is alive is the name we use when they are dead because the Language lives always. I said to my children Aniceta, Apolonia, and Aparicio, I said, Your father Nicanor will always be alive like his name which is alive in the Language and I told them all that on the same night another soldier arrived to give me money that Nicanor had sent from the war and I thought it must be a message from before, arriving after Nicanor died, and I went with my three children to find a place to set a wood cross next to an agave plant and put his name there on an empty grave. But then another day a different soldier came and told me, Nicanor is fine and sends you a message, and I asked, What happened, I didn't understand if it was truth or lies that Nicanor was dead or alive, but I went with my three children to make the wood cross with Nicanor's name on it next to the agave, to set it there with his name so we could go there to pray for him and for buds to sprout up there with his memory in them, but I didn't know if we had to put him in there dead or if it was just his name that would go there, so I went for some wood and made the cross with a nail and that's how we set his name in the earth. Then more money arrived and I cried because I didn't know if Nicanor was alive or dead, I didn't understand, I told my sister Francisca and I told Gaspar that I didn't understand, but I told my three children that their father died in the war, it was better if they believed that death had laid its egg in their father than if they believed me saying he was alive, how could my children believe me if I said that Nicanor was resurrected like Jesus Christ, but Aniceta understood I was crying because I didn't know what was truth and what was lies, Aniceta saw how confused I was about the wood I used to make the cross with Nicanor's name on it to set in the earth, not knowing if we were going to dig a hole to bury his body there where his name was already waiting and I told my three children, Nicanor's name on that cross is all we need, because there are no times or dates, the Language lives always. One day, another soldier came with money and told me that Nicanor had been killed in the war, and we went to cry for him at the wood I made into a cross with Nicanor's name on it and set in the earth, and that time I cried like a newborn cries, with relief, I cried for the hope he was alive but not long after that Nicanor showed up at our door, drunk. I didn't recognise him at first, with his ammunition belts and his rifle, his beard and clothing made him look like someone else and his sweat was sour with liquor.

When Nicanor came back from the war, his taste for liquor rotted our marriage the way a fruit rots if no one collects it from the ground. He lost his temper with me and our three children, my sister Francisca couldn't look him in the eye, she couldn't talk to him, and Gaspar who wasn't yet Paloma stopped coming to the house because Nicanor was a beast. He began to beat Aniceta, Apolonia, and Aparicio if they said something he didn't like and the next day he would feel guilty and ask for their forgiveness, he hit me a few times and he smashed one of Francisca's pots because he didn't like the atole she made that day, he said it tasted like dirt. He beat Aparicio with whatever he had on hand. Once, a young buck made Aparicio cry, Aparicio's lips were blue and his face was blue from so much crying, and Nicanor went to beat him because his son, his male son, was crying because of some kid and Men don't cry, he said, and he left Aparicio's lips bleeding and he knocked one of his teeth out, and I had to hold the tooth in place all night until it stuck back in its pod, when the sun came out from its mountain the tooth was back in its pod, the boy was crying from the pain and I packed some herbs around the hollow to soften the pain and held his tooth in its pod until it took root.

I realised that Nicanor had his eye on a girl and that he had started going with her at night. I realised it right away. Nicanor didn't die in the war, the messages the soldiers brought me killed him and resurrected him many times, he and his rifle fought with the revolutionaries and he came back drunk to San Felipe to go with that girl at night. Nicanor didn't die with those other men in the war, even though Aparicio says he did because Aparicio has no saint but Nicanor, and Nicanor died hacked to death with a machete by the girl's brother, Viviana was her name and he took her to a little hut at the far end of San Felipe. People said that Viviana went with him at night by force. But I'll tell you something that only time lets me say. If they had told me back then that Nicanor brought the girl to that hut to climb onto her by force, I would have hacked him to death with a machete myself, this is something lodged in me here like a sigh I can't let out, I carry it here lodged inside me always and it breaks me to talk about it because a man climbed onto my sister Francisca that way and I could do nothing to help her. And then I heard about what happened with Nicanor and Viviana. He didn't climb onto her by force, they went together at night, Nicanor didn't climb onto her by force but I would have pulled him off her myself and hacked him to death with a machete if he had, because of the man who did that to my sister Francisca.

My sister Francisca told me what had happened after she had her first moon and before I was married and I saw it years later in a ceremony I made for my sister after I received the Book, the one my father had spoken about before he died and the one Gaspar said I would have, before he was Paloma, there in the ceremony I saw the wretch climb onto my sister by force and I tell you I could have killed him myself with a machete, and still to this day because memory doesn't quiet the rage. I don't kill, I don't do people harm, but I feel rage against that wretch and so I say I could have killed him, may God forgive me for saying it. It was in the milpa, it was right over there. My sister Francisca had just had her first moon and she made waters on our sleeping mat, sometimes that happened to her at night, I saw that and before I was married to Nicanor I told my sister Francisca, you're a woman now, what are you doing, go outside to do that. During the day she went outside, but at night sometimes she still wet herself. Even before Francisca had her first moon her breasts were already like sweet fruits and she was always taller than me, who knows how because my mother was short like I am and my grand-mother Paz was even shorter, shorter than my mother and me, and my grandfather Cosme was short, too, but people respected him because of how he was and because of the way he treated people, he looked them in the eye and remembered the things they'd said and he knew all their names and what they'd talked about the last time he saw them, my grandfather Cosme was short like us and my sister Francisca, God knows how, was taller than us the way one stalk can grow taller than the rest of the corn no matter how hard the wind shakes it, and she grew quickly into a woman's body, and all the men watched her when she walked through the town, they said things to her. I remember Gaspar who wasn't yet Paloma said to her that she was beautiful and painted her lips but my sister Francisca wiped her lips clean with a rag because she didn't want people to see her so much like a woman. Before I was married I saw that my sister Francisca was wetting herself in her sleep and I woke her and said to her, Francisca, go get some rags to clean this, you're a woman now and too old to be doing this and she began to cry and didn't say a word and I went to get the rags so she wouldn't get a caning across her hands. I did that other times, too, and went to buy a new mat so no one would say anything to her, I changed the new mat for the old one and no one noticed, that's how she came to tell me what happened to her, and later I saw it in a ceremony.

The wretch stuck his fat, dirty fingers in my sister Francisca by force, it burned and she wanted to be anywhere else but there was no one to help her, her breasts were bare to the harsh sun burning white in the sky, she could hardly speak because she wanted to be anywhere else and didn't understand why he was sticking his dirty fingers in her, she wanted to escape from that wretch and his fingers cracked from ploughing but he didn't stop and she couldn't escape, he was holding her down with the breasts of her woman's body bare but she wanted to be anywhere else, not with that wretch who was telling her in her ear that she was going to thank him one day after she was married off with her bride price, that she was going to remember him on her wedding night, that she was going to remember how big he was, but what was big was my sister Francisca's terror, and the wretch forced her, he told her many times that she would always remember him, that no one would ever give it to her like he did, and he forced himself inside her and it hurt and Francisca wanted to be anywhere else when he stuck his fingers inside her with his dirty nails and his putrid soul and he grabbed her breasts, breasts even she never touched when she washed in the mornings before the sun came out of its mountain so she didn't have to see her woman's body, with her big black eyes and her long black hair that she scrubbed with reeds to make it shine, and while it was happening my sister Francisca rested her mind on a painting hung next to Christ in the town church, a painting of a white Virgin with her white feet floating in the clouds and the clouds look like they're moving, like the ones that blow through on clear afternoons when the sky is clean and freshly washed blue, fat white clouds like children fat and red-cheeked with breast milk, Because those clouds took me to another place, Feliciana, she said, a place where she was safe inside the smell of white flowers in the town church, and she felt the cool of its floor and its shade on hot days, my sister Francisca saw the Virgin and felt her feet in those fat white clouds like children fat and red-cheeked with breast milk, clouds that smell like milk like newborn babies smell, and she thought about how feet must feel in those soft white clouds, lighter than air, and my sister Francisca smelled the milk scent of newborn babies and she felt peace while the wretch licked her breasts like fruit that belonged to him and drooled the rank pulque of his soul all over them.

There are wretches who have no name, there are wretches in the Bible, wretches in every town, wretches in every tongue and every time and women will keep birthing them, but for me none of them will ever have a name, because their name is the name of their crime. My sister Francisca is a woman with a clean and quiet soul and has been since the day she was born. I wouldn't be Feliciana if I didn't have my sister Francisca, just like you wouldn't be who you are without your sister Leandra. Sisters are what we are not, they have what we don't and we are what they are not.

Nicanor didn't climb onto Viviana by force. A few years later Apolonia came to tell me that Viviana was pregnant from her husband, she had four children with her husband, and Aniceta and Apolonia held bitterness toward Nicanor because they heard people in town say that their father was a drunk who had gone at night with Viviana, but I said to them, Nicanor gave you life, don't hold spite toward him because nothing grows from burnt seeds, girls, flowers most certainly don't, those won't grow if your father's name is burnt. You have a husband and a son, so you understand. I told my children, Nicanor gave you life so don't hold spite toward him, go to where he is buried under the cross I made with a nail to plant his name in the earth, go pray to the name of your father Nicanor, go to the wood cross to share your pain and your joy because he gave you life. One day Viviana came to see me because her cousin had pains of the liver, and Viviana told me that she had known other men before Nicanor and that she had wanted to run away with him, that they had gone together at night because it was what she wanted, that he hadn't climbed onto her by force but her brother hacked Nicanor to death with his machete because he thought his sister was there by force, she told me that she felt guilt towards me and wanted to tell me and also that she wanted me to heal the pains troubling her cousin's liver. I helped Viviana's cousin, I healed her cousin's liver and I tell you, in this land the sun shines a light on all it touches, Viviana told me that she had brought Nicanor to her house with her, that he was drunk and her brother didn't know she was already going with men at night, that Nicanor had the bad luck of being the first one her brother found out about and the boy thought Nicanor had climbed onto her by force.

10

I hadn't said anything about it, but Feliciana knew. Some piece of shit had abused Leandra when she was sixteen. It was right after my father's death, and my mother was putting in extra hours at the university; when she got home, she'd turn on the television and sit in front of it until she fell asleep. Her temperament wasn't depressive, it never had been. She didn't sink into the couch and sob after my father died, but during that period she did watch one documentary after another, completely absorbed by what was happening on-screen. If the documentary was about something that had nothing to do with her life, she'd be even more into it. My mother didn't want fiction, she wanted reality – but a reality distant from her own. On my father's birthday, two and a half months after he died, Leandra and I were in the kitchen making quesadillas when my mother told us we couldn't imagine everything that went on in the expanding universe, and explained to us in detail how she thought black holes should be measured. It was my father's birthday, but none of us could say the words. My mother started watching a series about outer space – the Milky Way, the galaxy, physics and big philo-sophical questions; at one point, I noticed that she'd changed the photo backdrop on her office computer from a picture of the four of us on a trip to one of an astronaut floating in space. I think it was the perfect self-portrait for her at the time.

The older sister of one of Leandra's friends at the open education college she went to after getting kicked out of three other schools was a dentist. She was a cheerful, chatty twenty-nine-year-old with dimpled cheeks and a way of speaking that I found welcoming; she was always ready to talk about some current event – the more pop the topic, the more involved she got and the harder she laughed, and I always enjoyed her company when I'd stop by to pick up my sister or drop her off. One time, Leandra was having dinner at her friend's house and mentioned she was looking for a job. The friend's sister suggested a two-week trial, it just so happened they were looking for a receptionist at her practice. Leandra didn't know the first thing about nursing or dentistry, but the kid who managed the appoint-ment calendar and handled administrative tasks had quit a few days earlier. That was Leandra's first job, and it was the closest she'd ever get to a career in medicine, since ironically she couldn't stand the sight of blood. She had no problem tossing a grenade if something rubbed her the wrong way, like when she set a fire at her school, but blood was too much. I was shaken when I heard about the fire, but not surprised. No one was injured and it didn't make the evening news, but the outcry reached other schools and my parents' co-workers. Leandra was someone who could make a statement with an act of arson, but who'd nearly pass out if she cut her finger while slicing a lime.

Sometimes Leandra would wear a smock that had a grinning mouthful of teeth with braces on it, and sometimes she'd wear one with balloons in different shades of blue. They tended to clash with her personality and style, which had nothing to do with uniforms or brand names. In the months that followed my father's death, Leandra started losing weight like a bar of soap melting away. She went from curvy to skinny in a matter of weeks. Of the three of us, Leandra was most in touch with her feelings of loss: she cried or blew up at the drop of a hat, we never knew which version of her would greet us in the morning. She was carried along on the currents of her mood, which could take her in any direction, but most of the time she was angry. She would tell anyone who'd listen what she remembered about our father, she remembered him out loud and was the only one of us three who spoke her mind right away. In other words, of us three, she had the best digestive system.

It's funny how the cards fall in a family – the actors change, but the roles stay the same. My mother, who had always been the talkative one, spent those days inside her shell, while Leandra, who'd always been more closed off and sarcastic suddenly became the sincere, loquacious one. My mother and I found shelter in our work. I threw myself into my studies and my job at the newspaper. Into my denial, that is.

One Friday morning, I ran into Leandra in the bathroom and she told me she was planning to go to a party that night. I was at the newsroom going through some handwritten edits my boss had left me when my mother called my cell phone to say she was on her way to pick me up. I told her I couldn't leave, that I was in the middle of work, but her tone worried me; she said she'd pick me up in fifteen minutes so I could show her how to get to the house of a kid named Fernando, one of Leandra's friends. I'd just met a new hire at work named Julian, who had a skateboard and a gap between his front teeth. I called my sister a few times, but her phone was off. My mother didn't pick up, either. I hadn't spoken with Julian much, but he seemed like a decent guy. I felt like I could tell him I thought something serious was up with my sister; he didn't ask a single question and told me not to worry about anything at the office.

We got to Fernando's house. My mother rang the buzzer until he answered; he told her Leandra wasn't there, but my mother didn't give up. A neighbour opened the front door before Fernando could answer again and she forced her way in. She came out a few minutes later with a very drunk Leandra. When my sister got in the car, she started crying and said she didn't feel well. I got into the back seat with her, opened the door, and held her hair while she vomited. We got home after stopping twice more for me to hold my sister's hair. My mother didn't say a word. I could feel her adrenalin surging. I had thought we were picking Leandra up because she was wasted, I'd assumed she had called my mother, but I soon learned that it had been my mother's intuition that had sent her looking for Leandra. Leandra was very drunk and her phone had died, and she hadn't sent my mother Fernando's address. I'd taken her to his house a few times, so I knew how to get there. She could barely string a sentence together, more because of her emotional state than because of the alcohol. I sensed that they knew something I didn't, and asked my mother to tell me what was going on. Your sister should tell you, Zoe, she said as she opened the car door. For the first time in her mourning, she went inside and didn't turn on the documentary channel. Instead, she went into her room and I heard the radio tuned to a news station we hadn't listened to since my father died. I brought my sister to our room, sat on the corner of her bed, and brushed her fringe away from her forehead. She was sweating.

Leandra said she'd only drank one beer and a mezcal,

and had felt tired. She and Fernando were planning to go to a party afterward, but she'd fallen asleep. It was just the two of them. Leandra had thought it was strange to be so tired after just two drinks, and had laid down when she felt a hand rubbing her back. She asked Fernando to let her sleep for a little and said that she was dizzy. She still wanted to go to the party and thought she'd feel better after a quick nap. She was also a little disoriented and still couldn't understand why she felt so tired, or why the fuck Fernando kept rubbing her back; she thought maybe she'd eaten something that didn't agree with her, maybe her tolerance had gone down since she'd lost weight. My sister asked Fernando not to touch her, but he ignored her and wrapped his arms around her from behind and kissed her neck, he grabbed her breasts through her shirt and tried to take it off; half unconscious, she struggled to tell him please, stop. He grabbed her nipples through her shirt; with what little strength she had, she managed to get his hands off her and told him not to get the wrong idea, that she needed to sleep a little, that she wasn't interested in him. But he didn't stop, he said that she was the one who'd gotten into his bed and then he said she was probably a virgin as he wrapped his arms tighter around her from behind. She asked him to stop touching her and he told her to knock it off, he knew she liked it. My sister felt queasy and her body weighed a tonne. She must have passed out for a few minutes when she felt his erection against her thigh and moved away. She was wearing a skirt. In a single movement, he pulled her underwear to the side and she felt his erection between her legs. Who knows where she found the strength, but Leandra managed to get up and run to the bathroom, and with the last of her energy she locked the door. From the bed, Fernando said that was proof she was a virgin. Leandra sat on the bathroom floor while Fernando kept taunting her. She guessed he was masturbating from what he was saying. That was when the doorbell rang, and she knew it was my mother.

My sister hadn't had any intention of leaving that bathroom. She knew Fernando would get bored eventually and would go to the party. She knew that if he locked her in, she could climb through the kitchen window to a spiral staircase that led to the parking area. But she was frightened. On the other side of the door, that prick Fernando was still taunting her about being a virgin, about how she dressed in black like a nun, how she dressed weird. You're too hot to dress like a fucking weirdo, he'd said, followed by, You're missing out on this good shit, bitch, while in the bathroom my sister was asking herself what the fuck he'd put in her mezcal. Her body felt heavy and her vision was blurred.

When I asked my mother, she said she'd had an intuition. Given the time, she'd figured they would still be at that piece of shit's place. She was furious; it was the first time since my father's death I'd seen her so present, like a meteorite fallen to earth. I think she came back from outer space when she gave that prick Fernando what he had coming and got Leandra out of there. My mother suggested that Leandra press charges. Leandra didn't want to.

She fell asleep late that night and woke up twice; a few nights of insomnia followed, along with two panic attacks. After that, Leandra had a hard time being inside an elevator, a car, any small, enclosed space; at parties she always checked where the exits were, and she said to me once that MRI machines seemed worse than anything she'd seen in any horror film. That night she woke me up; she threw something and went to pick it up, then asked me if I'd ever wondered where our mother's intuition came from. She said my father once told her that our mother had woken him up in the middle of the night to say that his uncle had just died in an accident on the highway to Cuernavaca. This was before cell phones. My father, shaken, called his uncle's house to see how everyone was; his aunt picked up the phone and said that his uncle was on a trip. Not long after, my father's cousin called to say that his uncle had died on the highway to Cuernavaca. Another time, my mother told me that there hadn't been ultrasounds back when Leandra and I were born, and that she'd thought I was going to be a boy for a few months, until one night she had a dream about me: I found you on a park bench, she said, with your face covered in mud. I cleaned you up. In my dream, you looked exactly like you did when you were two, and I knew you were my daughter. I woke your father up and told him: We're going to have a little girl, and she's going to look just like you.

The next morning, my mother was pruning the living room plants, something I normally did. Leandra was hungry and was going through the containers in the fridge to see if there were any leftovers she might want to eat. Remembering what Leandra had told me in the middle of the night, I asked my mother how she'd known to go to that piece of shit's house, where the impulse had come from.

"All women," she said, dropping the dead leaves into a small plastic bag, "are born with a bit of bruja in them, for protection."

"But we were the ones who went for Leandra, Mum."

"Who said anything about protecting yourself, all by yourself? Though, who knows, the thing with your father's uncle scared me. I wasn't protecting anyone then, so I guess I don't really have a theory. All I know is that I felt something. That time, I just had a premonition and told your father to check on your great uncle. But sadly, yes, I'd seen his death."

"How did you see it?"

Leandra didn't want to talk about what had happened

the night before, and my mother made it clear that she planned to follow her lead.

"I don't know . . . the same way certain thoughts come without your calling them up. They're moments of clarity you don't second guess."

"And what did you feel yesterday, exactly?" Leandra asked.

My mother avoided going into detail; she wanted Leandra to feel comfortable saying whatever she wanted, whenever she wanted, but she also needed to understand where her daughter was at the moment.

"I had an instinct, same as I think any mother would if her cub were in danger."

That afternoon, Leandra and I went out to eat for the first time in forever. We got tacos and Leandra ate more than I did. It seemed like a vital response. We walked along a street lined with shops: a hardware store, a bodega, several clothing stores, a shop that sold orthopedics and looked like it was trapped in the seventies, and a few others. Leandra stopped at the window of a record store, and we talked about the album covers on display. She'd linger over the ones that had a design element or some use of colour that caught her eye; she knew a bit about who had designed a few of them, something I'd never thought about. I'd even go so far as to say her taste in music was connected to these visuals. Leandra knew about illustrators, photographers, and artists involved in album design; what little I knew, I'd learned from her. None of that stuff mattered to me, and I didn't particularly care about owning the physical albums.

The differences between us were also obvious in the way we dressed. From the time she was little, Leandra almost always wore black – black jeans or a black skirt, crewneck T-shirt or a black cotton sweater and black boots. She had five bags that had been made by hand in different communities. I remember a Wayuu bag in neon colours that one of my mother's co-workers brought back for her from Colombia after the two of them had a long conversation about things made by hand, and another bag that had been woven from raw wool by Zapatista women. She had a few strange pieces that she wore with attitude: a grey tunic cut like a giant rubbish bag that she wore with a black belt, a kimono, an African dashiki she'd bought from a street vendor downtown, and a yellow skirt from Oaxaca that she wore like a minidress. The fact was, Leandra could have thrown on a towel or a curtain and given it shape with that black belt, and she would have pulled it off because she wore everything with confidence.

She was vocal in her criticism of transnational corporations, those giant monopolies whose employees worked under precarious, inhumane conditions. She never bought anything from a chain store, and whenever my mother or I did Leandra would drone on for hours about how those places treated workers and about children in floating sweatshops. My father wasn't interested in clothing so Leandra never regaled him with one of her sermons, but I told him about them and he respected her position, even if it seemed radical to him. People always used to ask her where she'd bought something, because she tended to shop in places most teenagers didn't know about. Even for something as simple as a black sweater: Leandra had probably gone to buy a few skeins of wool and paid the elderly ladies of a local knitting club a fair price to make it for her. I didn't care much about clothing: I wore light, neutral colours and if I saw something in a store that I liked I'd buy it if could afford it, but it wasn't anything I paid attention to. Like our mother, Leandra enjoyed putting an outfit together, whereas I would've been fine with wearing a uniform. Come to think of it, I think my father actually did make a uniform for himself, with two or three chromatic variations.

Leandra dressed almost exclusively in black when she was sixteen. She's always been into geometric patterns, handmade bags. She liked bright lipstick and nearly always had her lips painted, like my mother. When she was seven, she loved colourful pens and had a collection of letterhead that she'd taken from all over, starting with my parents' offices, even though she didn't like writing letters. She didn't like to write at all, for that matter: she used her school notebooks for drawing geometric patterns. Back then, she loved little animal stamps, especially of cats. At seven, she said that if she were an animal, she'd be a cat, and then cracked up while telling me I'd be a dog. When she was little, she loved going to stationery stores and she loved the smell of those notebooks with plastic covers, though she was bored stiff by everything that went into them, by their reason for existing, and – while we're at it – by the educational system as a whole. One day, after she'd already been kicked out of three schools, she said to me, The problem, Zoe, isn't Jesus Christ, he's fine; the problem is Christians. This was the same person who'd begged me to take Holy Communion with her. It's the same thing with schools, she went on. Education isn't the problem; the problem is the teachers who treat us like idiots.

One time, when she was around fourteen, she informed me with complete conviction that she was getting a tattoo the minute she could. Our father had asked us to wait until we were eighteen. She got her first tattoo on her eighteenth birthday: three rectangles in primary colours. When I asked her what it meant, she said, Why do tattoos always have to mean something? It looks cool, doesn't it?

By fifteen, Leandra was completely fascinated by form and colour; she'd spend hours staring at things, imagining herself as a designer one day. She couldn't have cared less about books. She opened one in a bookstore once, read the first page out loud, and said to me, I don't get why you like this stuff, Zoe. Who the fuck talks like this? In museums, the more abstract a colourful composition was, the more it interested her. If the image hung from the thread of some anecdote, Leandra would cut that thread with a razor-sharp phrase. In fact, she loved slicing through arguments like the strings on a puppet; in part, that was the problem she had with authority. She was interested in the image, and only the image. I was the opposite: at museums, I often spent more time reading the descriptions of artworks than looking at the art itself. As Feliciana says, our sisters are everything we aren't. That day, as we walked into the record store, she asked me if I thought she'd ever design something a stranger would look at in a shop window, like we were doing, and would like it enough to discuss it with the person they were with.

Not long after turning fifteen, Leandra shaved her head. She went into a barber shop and asked them to buzz her hair off like a soldier's. When my mother saw her, she said she'd look great no matter what she did to her hair. My father saw it as an act of aggression, of anger at the world, but he didn't say anything to me about it until a few weeks after Leandra's hair had begun to grow back. Leandra realised he was biting his tongue and calmly said to him one evening in the garage, as he was oiling some car part by the light of a small lamp, that there was no reason to associate long hair with femininity, which took many forms. My father gave her a kiss and told her that she could do whatever she liked. Those two never talked much but they were deeply connected in their silence, like snails.

Both Leandra and my father liked spaces more than things. She hated going into stores and had strong opinions about capitalism; it was like trying to shop with a preacher who never shut up, and sometimes it was easier just to leave her at home. When she did set foot in a store, though, she was less interested in the objects for sale than in how they were arranged in the displays. She liked old cafés, old buildings, and fruit and flower stands where she'd linger, chatting with the vendors even if she wasn't going to buy anything; she had my mother's skill with people and my father's soft touch, all of which contrasted starkly with how categorical, cutting and earnest she could be when confronting an injustice. Leandra hated bullying of any kind, and any racist, classist, xenophobic attitude aimed at silencing someone or putting them at a disadvantage. That was a one-way ticket to her violent side, to the rage that led her to start a fire in the third school that expelled her when she was thirteen.

Leandra had a record of bad conduct, and even though she seemed like a seriously troubled teen, there was something deep down in her way of being that convinced my parents she'd find her place in the world. She liked geometric patterns, so she began taking photos of the shapes she found in the street with the camera my father gave her after the fire. She also liked to watch the street being cleaned. Near where we lived, there was a woman who played her radio full blast while she washed the sidewalk in front of her house every morning; she did her work with passion, singing and scrubbing with a bucket of water beside her. My sister took a series of photographs of the woman, and one time she said to me, Look, Zoe, the circles she makes on the ground in water change depending on the music. Leandra always made friends wherever she went. I remember she got out of the car once to buy coffee and came back saying we were going out that night, that the person in line behind her had invited us to a party. Of the two of us, Leandra was always the one who had a big group of friends, it didn't matter if she only lasted five minutes at a school, that was enough for her to secure social plans and promises of invitations to come. After the fire she started when she was thirteen, though, she began to spend more time with the camera my father gave her.

Leandra has always hated her birthday. To this day, I still hear her ask people not to celebrate it; she hates cake and "Las mañanitas", and thinks that wishing someone a happy birthday demeans us as a species. She started hating birthday parties when she was ten or eleven years old.

She thinks they're cheesy. Even now, she lies about her birthday, moving it a few days earlier or later, so that if someone wishes her a happy one at least their aim is off. She looks pained in all the photos my mother ever took of her at parties, like someone had forced her into it – just like my father, who hated having his picture taken. He preferred to be the one behind the camera, and so does Leandra.

I was into dark films and tabloid rags, and Leandra got the giggles during horror films; in real life, though, things were totally different: Leandra couldn't stand the sight of blood and I was easily frightened. She wasn't a prude, but I was. If she was proud of anything it was her body, as a chubby little girl or as a slim teenager, whereas I was shy all through my adolescence. Leandra would shit with the door open and if I said anything about it as I passed, she'd chew me out for being there in the first place. She fainted once, around the time she lost all that weight. I wasn't with her when it happened, but that kind of physical weakness or vulnerability seemed at odds with her personal strength. In that, she was like our father. Despite what happened, Leandra put on a brave face about the incident with that piece of shit Fernando. The day after it happened, we went out to eat tacos and wander around, and her attitude made it clear that she wanted to come out of the whole thing stronger.

That afternoon we spent strolling around aimlessly, she told me about a big abandoned building on Insurgentes with a bunch of smashed windows and graffiti all over it; she said it was like a large bird with short wings, a nuisance among functional structures. But I guess that happens in the best of families, Zoe. Leandra liked old buildings, with their damaged façades, their dirty windows, their battered doors, their metal fixtures eaten away by time. She liked Mexico City's buildings from the seventies: the colourful tiles arranged in seemingly random patterns in the lobby, the metalwork, the giant windows in those spacious apartments, the afternoon sun forcing its way through the curtains. Leandra once told me she was curious about the city where our parents had been young. A few days after the incident with Fernando, she began a photo series of buildings from the seventies, maybe as a way to get closer to my father. After all, he'd been the one who'd given her the camera – he'd seen something in her that even she hadn't sensed yet.

My father took pictures of objects, houses, places, abandoned cars and bridges – almost never of people. If a person appeared in one of his photos it was like an accident, something unavoidable, the way a tree or a pile of bricks might sneak into the frame in someone else's family album. Our photo albums were full of my father's pictures of places and things; the few pictures they contained of people were ones my mother had taken or the Polaroids she often bought from event photographers. In that sense, their taste in photography was a translation of my father's and my mother's way of being. For her, if the picture didn't have smiling faces in it, it had to be taken again: everyone in the frame, with their arms around one another.

Leandra started taking pictures of buildings from the seventies because they made sense to her, in their way, and because she imagined my father had walked past them at some point. She found ones she thought my father might have liked as much as she did, like a child inventing a game with straws and napkins at a table full of adults. She took a bunch of photos. Doorways without doormen, spaces where – decades ago – a desk had stood with a chair and a small black-and-white television. Entryways adorned with fake plants and the occasional person passing through. Even today, those buildings make me think more of Leandra than of my father. Actually, they make me think of how Leandra saw my father.

Between her time at the open education college and her job as a receptionist at a dentist's office where she wore a uniform that made her look like another person, Leandra went out and took these pictures, developed them, and sometimes asked for my opinion. I wondered if she was fascinated by what happened in those spaces, behind the windows – which was the thing I was most curious about. She said it never even occurred to her. I think that's one of the things that made us different as teenagers, and continues to now.

These are some of the things Leandra liked. She disliked, on the other hand, eighties houses with stucco walls, modern buildings that looked like stacks of white shoeboxes, banks, and drug stores, which she found visually horrifying. She despised opulent structures that flaunted their luxuries. There was an old pharmacy downtown that she went to now and then to buy brown glass bottles in different sizes, like the ones they'd use at the chemist's – that was how she marked her things as separate from mine in the bathroom we shared. The pharmacy had been using the same ticket system to place orders for a century and there were always long lines to pay. She liked that they sold essential and natural oils, along with bases like glycerine and alcohol, and used them to make her own face masks, soaps, perfume, and shampoo. I asked her once how she came up with a gorgeous perfume she was wearing, and with a massive grin she said to me, Those big companies can go fuck themselves, sis, we're not all going to smell the same. We're not mannequins on some assembly line, whose fucked-up idea was that?

She's always hated the tabloids, with their close-ups of dead bodies in a pool of blood under a supposedly clever headline; she disliked it when people talked about dramatic accidents, and she had a hard time whenever someone would go into detail about an illness or some mishap that involved blood. When we met my parents at the hospital before the second heart attack that took my father's life, a nurse had left a soft plastic tube hanging and a yellowish liquid dripped onto the floor; it wasn't clear if the fluid was coming out of my father or if it was medicine, but Leandra had to step out for a moment. She was really shaken up, she hated the sight of blood. My father had shared his taste for cold cuts with me, and it warms my heart to see Felix brings pieces of chorizo to his mouth, since my father enjoyed grilling on Sundays; I know that if he were still with us, he'd happily trade bites with his grandson.

Leandra also hated rats when she was little, she was terrified of them. She had no problem making a molotov cocktail in our bathroom, to defend an ideal, but was completely defenceless when it came to rats. She couldn't stand the sight of them, but she liked snakes and even asked for one as a pet when she was eleven, a water snake she set free in our room when I wasn't there – it made my skin crawl, despite its withdrawn serpentine demeanor. She didn't like rodents or cockroaches, but she was happy watching the snake slither across the carpet in our room for hours on end, and enjoyed making little obstacle courses for it.

I liked reading scary stories when I was a teenager, I enjoyed the suspense. Leandra never cracked a book unless she had to, but she had a good memory for the dialogue in films she liked. She liked to recite that famous monologue from *The Exorcist* like she was that little possessed girl; cackling with laughter, she never missed an opportunity to do it. The sharpness of Leandra's memory always surprises me, she starts talking about some day in the distant past and mentions details I'd completely forgotten, like the plot of films we'd watched when we were little, when I can't even remember their titles, or whether I saw them or not in the first place. Manuel and I went through a rough patch before Felix was born, and we separated for a few months. I moved in with Leandra and her partner Tania, and the first thing she said to me over beers the night I arrived was, I always forget you're straight, Zo. That's why you have all these relationship problems. Bad jokes aside, I was always surprised by my sister's ability to remember even the smallest details of things.

She was introduced to horror films when we were kids. No one in our household had any particular interest in the genre. My father liked biopics and historical films, and my mother was happy to watch whatever the rest of us wanted. At school one time, some kids were talking about a film that had to do with a cemetery for pets; Leandra hadn't seen it, so they took turns telling her how it went. She came home that day bursting to tell me about how the animals would come back from the dead all satanic after being buried. And even though plenty of time had passed, when her water snake got lost in the house – even though my father told her that it was probably just curled around something in our room – Leandra clung to him for dear life until they found it coiled around the leg of her bed. She often spent hours locked in our room, drawing, while I was playing the drums. I don't know exactly when, but Leandra was maybe eleven when she developed a crush on a friend of hers named Lalo. Leandra didn't say anything about her crush, but one night she told me, from her bed to mine, that he went to Tepoztlán every weekend with his parents, and that he'd go off with the daughter of one of their friends to experiment with all the things Leandra hadn't thought kids could do. I think these stories about her friend stirred something in Leandra she'd never felt before: her burgeoning hormones.

The next morning as we were brushing our teeth she said, with her mouth still full of toothpaste, But I didn't even tell you the whole story . . . They went swimming together NAKED, Zoe. NAKED. Their parents had gone out to dinner and they'd stayed behind in the pool and since there was no one around THEY TOOK OFF THEIR BATHING SUITS and kept swimming. Leandra's eleven-year-old mind was blown by this, and so was mine.

Without saying anything to me or my father, she'd pulled a few photos out of the white boxes where he kept the pictures he'd taken over the years, and she'd written a letter to Lalo on the letterhead she collected. She gave him the Zippo Spectrum she always carried in her backpack. Lalo smoked, and she was convinced he'd make better use of it. She gave him the letter, and he stopped talking to her. One day, someone told her that he'd laughed at her for giving him photos of empty spaces and had said it seemed like witchcraft, not to mention the fact she'd declared her love for him. All she said to me was, Now I'm out one Zippo and a friend, sis, I guess that's what love is – you give all you've got and the other person just keeps it, like it's no big deal. A few days later, Lalo gave her back the letter and the Zippo. That was one of the few times Leandra got her heart broken. But even after the Fernando incident, she found ways to transform a moment of vulnerability into strength.

Lalo was fourteen at the time, and Leandra never sought him out again after he returned the Zippo and the letter. He liked to brag about his conquests, and she heard a rumour that he counted her as one. Leandra started going out with a neighbour she liked, who treated her well and was head over heels for her, but she didn't pay much attention to him. It'd be fair to say that my sister understood how she wanted to be treated in a relationship very early on. She had a boyfriend much earlier than I did. My parents reacted to the news by imposing old-fashioned rules on us, something we hadn't expected, given their general open-mindedness. From then on, my father gave us a curfew.

The afternoon Leandra and I spent strolling around was nice. But my stomach clenched when I noticed how long she spent in the shower that night, and realised she was probably letting the water run over her while she thought about the incident with that piece of shit Fernando.

II

According to tradigion, a curandera should not have sexual relations with men and whoever takes the mushroom should not have sexual relations for five days before and five days after the ceremony, those who wish to can wait seven days. I didn't eat mushrooms during my marriage to Nicanor because I didn't want him to think I was a witch and because the rule about sexual relations must be honoured. At the end of my first year as a widow, I was clean and had no husband or any other man, but I had pains in one hip that no curandero could heal me of, so I decided to go to the hillside between San Juan de los Lagos and San Felipe where my father brought me before he died, where my sister Francisca and I went to tend the sheep and the goats, and there I found the same mushrooms that Gaspar, who was now Paloma, had touched the gentle way she touched everything, as if everything was a flower, sometimes you wished she would touch you, I had never seen that kind of gentleness before and much less when it came to touching, a person, I mean, I had never seen the kind of gentleness as the way Paloma touched the mushrooms before she gave them to my grandmother Paz in the ceremony that healed her. I carefully picked a few unions of mushrooms, because you eat them that way, in holy union, because just like in marriages they have to be loving couples where one gives strength to the other, and I pulled them gently from the ground as if they were dandelions among the grasses and treated them with care, as if they might fall apart and be scattered by the wind if I didn't hold them gently, and I remembered how Gaspar who was now Paloma held them, and I spoke to them and asked God to help me choose them and I chose them in unions because they are eaten that way, two at a time, and I went to heal myself in a ceremony that I made when my sister Francisca and my mother and my children were asleep. My mother was still with us, then. I thought if I can heal myself tonight then I can heal other people, because that's how it is with everything, first yourself, and then others, what you are able to do in your own deep waters you can do for others. And if I could do something to help others, then the blessings of my grandfather Cosme would be with me and I could share them with other people.

Back then I never thought I could stop working because hunger was always in our house and we were many mouths. I taught my children how to raise silkworms, like my sister Francisca and I did with my grandfather Cosme, and even though we didn't have the wares from before, I knew that silk is always good to sell. My mother and my sister Francisca were in charge of the milpa, of the coffee, of the squash and the beans that we grew. I did some of everything but my son Aparicio had ants in his pants, he never ever stopped moving, he had ants in his pants because he was the only man in the family after Nicanor died, you know how boys are in a family of women and we were nothing but women at home, like a little ant that boy went all around looking for a family of men to run off with, I think. My sister Francisca and I were obedient, curious but obedient, and she followed me everywhere, wherever I went there she was too, but she was calmer than me, and when Aparicio was born swollen and crying and with hair all over him, even on his backside because he was born hairy as a colt, I realised nothing was going to stop him from moving so I dug a hole next to the milpa, I dug a deep hole in the earth and that's where I put him so we could work in peace until he was old enough to understand that he had to work just like us. And I gave him a tortilla now and then and if he squealed I gave him some more and his sisters would help calm him down if he didn't go quiet. I would have dug three holes next to the milpa if my daughters hadn't let me work, but Aniceta and Apolonia were calm like my sister Francisca when they were little. Paloma gave Apolonia some of her shine later, but if there was one thing in that house it was work, and there is always a lot of work where there is hunger and many mouths and tetchy babies were a luxury we didn't have because tetchy babies get in the way. And that's why I tell my daughters that children in the city are used to things made for their size, as if the whole world were the size of their little hands, but children in the country have no choice but to do their duty in the same hole the adults use and their hands do the same work as adult hands because our world is a world of hunger and work.

My daughter Aniceta began making candles of pure beeswax and she made them in pairs so they could hang by their wicks from the ropes she strung between nails all around the house, and Apolonia made silk. From the time she started growing, you could tell Aniceta was going to change the ways of men, but she never let her eyes get dazzled by that and she enjoyed work, like my sister Francisca. My girl began making candles of pure beeswax in all sizes by the pair so the wicks could hang from the ropes strung around the house and she dyed some of the candles with cochineal and others with bark from the trees down in the gully, she got her gift for dyes from her great-grandmother, I told her, You got that from your great-grandmother Paz who used to make clothes for us and dyes from indigo and tree bark, your great-grand-mother Paz had two right hands for making clothes, and just like my mother had two right hands for embroidery, my daughter Aniceta made small candles and big ones for the altar so the church began to buy them from her, and so did the pastors and religious women, and women with plenty of coins to spend on their altars and their prayers. She was the one who began to provide for us with her candles of pure beeswax that she made in all sizes.

I was able to heal my own hip and so I knew I could heal other people, but I still didn't have the Book and I still didn't know what the Language could do, because that you don't know until God speaks to you like he spoke to me when he said, Feliciana this is your path. They say the darkest hour of night is when the sun is about to come out of its mountain, and that was how I began to do ceremonies, I healed my hip but for me the sun came out of its mountain when my sister Francisca got sick, until then I didn't know what the Language could do. After I healed my own hip, people would bring me their sick, a relative would ask me to heal their sick ones and I would heal them with herbs and with seven candles of pure beeswax that my daughter made, I healed with prayers and herbs and also with my hands. With my hands and my prayers I saw where the people's ills were and I cured people according to their ills with herbs I had blessed from the hillside. Paloma spread the word, she brought me an elder with fog over his eyes, at first people brought me elders. Paloma would drink liquor and tell me, Feliciana, love, God gave herbs and mushrooms to the poor to cure their ills and those are much more powerful than what they have in those city hospitals that only want to take people's coins. Paloma taught me how to talk with the herbs on the hillside, she went with me and with her smile and her humour she taught me how the herbs were like men and how the different kinds of mushrooms were like nights with men, it was Paloma who taught me to bless the herbs and the mushrooms.

I healed the elders who came to me with ills in their bodies, but I didn't yet know that I could heal ills of the soul. Back then few, very few people came to see me. Paloma could read a deck of cards to see the future in love and affections and so people would go to her when they had problems of the heart, since she was soft in the way she treated people and could make them laugh, people went to see her when they wanted to know their future, she also gave them advice about how to go with men at night and about their deep waters, but she wasn't a curandera anymore. I'm a bruja, love, she would say, call me the Red Witch, and she would laugh with her lips painted red.

I made my ceremonies with herbs I had blessed and sometimes with mushrooms, but more with the herbs, I made my herb mixtures and Paloma would say to me, Feliciana, you're like a mule without a lead, bring that over here, love, you need to put less of this, less of that, and more of this here, sweetheart. Paloma and I made the mixtures in buckets, and we tested them. We made medicines as mixtures that Paloma called Wine. Make more Wine for stomach aches, Feliciana, make more Wine for headaches, she'd say, make more Wine, Feliciana, for pains in the joints, and she would make Wine to calm inflammations of the liver, which people who enjoyed liquor welcomed. All the Wines did what they promised, and people wanted them. People from our towns have healed that way since the time of our ancestors, but Paloma and I did well with our Wines because the herbs had been blessed, because Paloma had a gift for choosing the herbs and for mixing them powerful and blessed.

To make the Wines, we mixed the herbs we had blessed in a bucket with alcohol and, depending on the illness, mint, salvia, rue, and cloves and whatever was missing we would go and find it while Francisca stayed with Aniceta, Apolonia, and Aparicio. People came because they heard I was from a family of male curanderos, but they didn't come to see me, they didn't come asking, Where's Feliciana, they said, They told me you come from a family of curanderos and that you could heal my sick one. Others came because they knew I made Wines with Paloma, and they said, That one is a man even though she's Muxe and she makes Wine because she comes from a family of male curanderos. Many rains passed before people remembered my name and came to see me. I said to them, I am a shaman,

I come from a family of wise men, but I am a woman and my name is Feliciana and I'm known in the heavens because God knows me, I am a woman who heals because mine is the Language.

You could say I was already a curandera of the Language because it is there in the deep waters and because I already knew the herbs and how to talk to them and how to make Wines to cure ills of the body, but my name hadn't yet travelled on the winds and I didn't yet have the Book. Not until my sister Francisca fell very sick, that was when my name grew on the wind because the wind multiplies. She would wake, stand up from her mat, go to the coffee crop and battle with her work, and she would fade there in the coffee crop until one day my daughter Apolonia cried, My aunt is dead! and I went out there, Aparicio wailed in his pit until Apolonia brought him water or carried him to cheer him up. My sister Francisca began to fade more often, the smallest effort made her fall flat out but she didn't want to pay attention to it, she never let her body rest and she never said anything to us. My son Aparicio threw a tantrum there once, squealed and squealed like a pig to make us take him out of the pit we dug so we could work in the milpa and plant our seeds, and I saw my sister Francisca fade, I saw her fall like a bag of stones. She said that her woman's time was coming but I looked at her and said, Francisca, it's too soon for that, and she said that her belly was caving in and shrivelling like a nut that had rotted because she never had children, she said that God was giving her the pains because she never had children, she paid no attention to her fading and said, This is what happens to women who don't have children because it is the will of God to dry their bellies like a nut. She kept working but she was fading more often and then one day she couldn't get up in the morning. She had no energy, she was slipping through like water slips through fingers.

I had already healed my own hip, and I healed a few elders who came to see me for Wine and praying because I come from a family of male curanderos who did good for people and the word spread because they were wise men and the people thought, We'll go to her because she is blood with the curanderos, but I was so sick with the sight of my sister Francisca and her sunken eyes, the hollows like black calabash cups, that I went to find Paloma so she would come heal my sister Francisca because I thought, She knows how, she healed my grandmother Paz. I found Paloma getting dressed in her Muxe clothing, with her long black hair almost blue she kept it so shiny, and the brooch she wore on the side where she had a scar on her brow. I put that brooch on her the day of her vigil, which was like a vela because people came from all over who loved Paloma, people loved her everywhere, and I put her brooch on her, on the side where she liked to wear it, she would say,

Feliciana, we don't hide our scars, we show them off. I'm proud of my low times, Paloma said, and she wore the brooch on that side because she liked it when people looked at her from that angle, from the side, and the brooch called the eye to the scar she had on her brow, it called the eye to her wound, and with her soft voice that seemed to touch things softly like I remembered Gaspar touching things and the hollows in her cheeks when she spoke because her voice in your ears was also a kind of touch, and soft, her voice was shiny like her hair so black it was blue, just like the night turns blue it gets so black, she was getting ready for a vela in another town, a dance they held every year where they would crown the Muxe Queen. Paloma was all dressed that night and she said to me, Feliciana, what's wrong, love, I'm getting pretty to go out with my girlfriends, what brought you here, sweetheart, you're as pale as flour. She was putting blue shine on her eyes, shine like she had on her hands when Guadalupe found her and came to tell me that they'd killed Paloma over there in front of the mirror, and there she was in front of that mirror where I saw her two times dead and she seemed two times alive, she was there when I went to see her to say help me with this terrible sickness that took hold of my sister Francisca. There were few Muxes in San Felipe then, now there are more, but then Paloma was one of the first to go where Muxes from all the towns got together for their velas. I had never seen anyone as sensual as Paloma, her hair so black it was blue with its shine and her brown skin with its shine, looking at her face brought pleasure like looking at the night sky free of clouds. Her eyes changed when she was not Gaspar anymore, Paloma's eyes held more joy, but her skin and her shine held the spirit of the boy who treated everything gently with his soft voice. I don't know why on that day I said to her, You look good, Gaspar. I wanted her to be Gaspar that day, I wanted her to be a curandero again because I needed her to answer me like a curandero, and she said, Feliciana, you must be joking, love, I'm Muxe, don't call me Gaspar because it sounds like you're gagging, sweetheart, call me Paloma because that's my name, I was born with wings, darling, why would you call me something so ugly as my father's name, my father who they say spent his life hardening his hands on the plough and sighing himself to death over his labours, the father I never knew except for a torn photo I found in my mother's things after she died, my father who I only knew through my mother's pain, Paloma fits me better, love, just like these beautiful clothes. Grandpa Cosme used to call me Pájaro but not because I walked like I had feathers, he called me that because I have wings where other people have regrets and fears and they can't stand up from the weight of everything their families expect from them, and to all those gentlemen I say, why carry around so many regrets and fears if Christ already carried them for you, my beauties, look at Him there on the cross suffering for you, go out and enjoy life because it is beautiful, and I say it with my lips painted red because otherwise my smile would be naked. Paloma was painting her lips and I needed her to help me like the time she healed my grandmother Paz, I saw her bring a miracle and I needed her to help me with my sister Francisca. Her lips were round like her round face and the red on them made her look beautiful because her soul was full of love and I called her Paloma then and never again called her Gaspar, I said, Paloma, you look beautiful with the blue gleam in your hair, in your eyes, with those red lips and that brooch calling the eye to your scar, and I never called her Gaspar again, and neither did my children or my sister Francisca because I asked them not to, and she said to me, Feliciana, we were all born to see beauty and to be happy, darling, but a sadness brought you here so tell me what's wrong, what has you pale as flour, and so while she painted herself in a mirror she had hanging from the wall I told her about my sister Francisca's sickness, I told her, I need you to help me heal her, Paloma, you're the only one who can bring the miracle, bring me a miracle like you did with my grandmother Paz, I asked her forgiveness for calling her Gaspar, I won't ever do it again, I said, and I saw in her face that she liked that, the hollows in her cheeks were deep and clear, the way they get when she's happy, it was as if my grandfather Cosme and my grandmother Paz and all the curanderos in my family and all the grandchildren I would have years later said to her at once, Paloma, you're beautiful, but she said to me, Feliciana, I stopped healing people a long time ago, I'm happy to help with the Wines and the herbs, love, but I can't help you with that, and I walked over to talk to her close while she painted herself and I smelled the liquor on her breath and saw that her lips had too much paint on them, that the paint spilled over the lines and that made her look more sensual, like someone who drinks too much liquor or spends too many coins at the market or stays too long in an embrace when saying goodbye, that was how her mouth looked, spilling over with red and all of her spilling over with blue shine and the shine of the hollows in her cheeks when she smiled. But in this emergency she was the only person who could help me and she had left the path of healing and nothing could bring her back because she had found her true path and it wasn't that of the curandero, it was her path as Paloma and when I saw her there flying, offering joy to the eyes of all who saw her gentle white flapping like she flapped her eyes when she put on her shine, when I saw Paloma flying I felt more alone in the world than ever before.

Paloma's house smelled of oils and perfumes because she was getting ready for the vela to see her girlfriends and for the coronation of the Muxe Queen. Her clothing and makeup and sparkles were all over the place, I had never seen clothing as sensual or makeup as colourful. My sister Francisca never cared about Sunday clothes, all the clothes we had were made of cotton and wool and made for working, and that was how it had always been. I never saw makeup or shine until my daughter Apolonia started wearing it to go into town, she was beautiful fresh from the bath but the makeup Paloma gave her looked good on her and Apolonia, who was the most like Nicanor, liked sensual clothing but only had two blouses for going out, my daughters didn't have any of the makeup or the clothing that Paloma had for the vela. That was a night for dances and eating in your best clothes and some Muxes braided their black hair with colourful ribbons, and others brushed their wet hair until it was straight, and others put curls in by rolling their hair around tubes the night before. They wore filigree earrings, they wore tehuanas and huipiles, they wore velvet skirts or lace, and some wore dresses from the city and spoke the government's tongue, but they all gathered at the vela to dance all night long and eat together. Paloma brought me to a few velas so I could sponsor the silk dress that the community would make for the Muxe Queen with Apolonia's silks, and that time I went to see her about my sister Francisca's sickness I realised that Paloma was the life of that festivity because while I was in her house helping her do up her dress I pictured her bringing life to the whole cantina with her soft voice, and the men who were happy listening to her voice and the things she said. Who wouldn't be happy seeing Paloma, she seemed like she had been born happy and was going to die happy, because if there was one thing Paloma enjoyed it was feeling good and that's how it was, exactly as I pictured her, even at her vigil. I also pictured my sister Francisca dead with her eyes sunken and sinking even more because death was going to lay its egg in her if I didn't heal her, and I went cold inside because I saw my sister Francisca dead with two heavy coins on her eyes to keep them from opening again. And because Paloma never missed anything, with the words that came out of her like flowers in spring, she said, Feliciana, don't pull that face, don't let those tears fall or you'll oversalt the beans, don't be upset, love, it's just that I don't do Children anymore, these days I do men.

Children was what Paloma called the mushrooms she used in the ceremonies, and as I watched her put makeup over the scar on her brow to make it stand out more, she said, You have to leave flowers on your battlefields, love. They gave her that scar when they saw how she swayed as she walked through the market, my grandfather Cosme said she walked like she had feathers and a man beat that scar into her brow when she was young, and as I watched her put makeup on that scar so it would stand out I thought how Francisca's eyes were going to sink more, that death was going to lay its egg if I didn't get there soon, those heavy coins were going to sink her eyes if I don't do something but I couldn't leave Paloma's house before I knew what to do to save my sister Francisca from death laying its egg in her and her eyes sinking deeper. Paloma took my face in her hands that smelled like church flowers, like the cream she had open in a little pot next to her mirror, and with her deep waters she looked at me and said, Feliciana, you have it, love, you just don't know it yet, I thought you knew, sweetheart. You'll be frightened because it's frightening to know the things you're capable of, dear, just picture what it must have been like for me when I was Gaspar, to bring someone back who was almost dead, you'll be frightened, love, like when you grab a scalding pot and you drop it in shock, that's the kind of fright you'll get when you see what you can do, the power you have inside is just as frightening as fire is to those who aren't expecting fire, and now picture if I told you that you were the one who heated the pot with your own fire, love, you'd shit yourself, dear. And I told her I didn't have time to think about any of that, that I healed my own hip and healed a few elders, but now I needed to heal my sister Francisca because she was going to die if I didn't save her and Paloma said to me, Well then, Feliciana, shake a leg, darling, go to the hillside, God is with you, love, the Language is yours and so is the Book, put yourself in God's hands for Him to help you, and so as I left her house I asked God to walk beside me on my path to choose the mushrooms and herbs on the hillside where my father took me before he died.

They say a man doesn't eat unless he is hungry, and that day I was determined to break the egg that death was bringing to my sister Francisca, I would not let death trill its song to her, I would take those coins from her eyes, those coins that already clouded her vision. I had healed myself, I had healed people who came to find me because I was blood with curanderos, I was afraid to fail but Paloma said to me, Feliciana, leave fear to the ingrates and the idiots, you have the Language deep inside you, and if you don't grab that pot once and for all it's the fire of guilt that will burn you, and it burns just as hot as the fire of fear. That night I thought, if this doesn't work, I'll repent until the day death lays its egg in me, but I knew that because I am blood with curanderos I could do what they did, and that I needed to do more because as a woman the flowers clean me as I walk and the waters clean me as I walk, I was born a woman and those powers don't change, life gives us its strength, I thought, the waters clean everything on the earth and they will make my path clean as I heal my sister Francisca who is so sick, because before that I had never healed someone who was between life and death.

And so that night I made a ceremony for the first time,

it was the first ceremony I made from my deep waters because you don't begin to walk the path of God until you're about to break, the sun comes out from its mountain when the night is darkest and I said I will watch the sun come out of its mountain and with my whole being I offered myself to God so I could heal my sister Francisca, and that was how I began to walk the path of my name when life asked it of me, and you could say that the other ceremonies were just practice because when you get sick anything could happen, but when someone you love suffers, those are the worst times and you grow old just thinking about the pain your loved one must be suffering. That night I wanted to take away the sickness that was sinking my sister Francisca's eyes and so I asked God to be at my side, and God listens when we call to him from our deep waters.

I lit the seven candles of pure beeswax that my daughter Aniceta had made, I prayed to God to take this sickness from both of us, from my sister Francisca and from me because when a relative you love is sick the cure is for the two of you and all the others of your blood, so I unwrapped the powerful unions of mushrooms from the piece of raw silk Apolonia gave me and as soon as I gave the unions of mushrooms to my sister Francisca she faded and that was when the mushrooms, which I started to call Children just like Paloma did, began to guide me. My sister Francisca opened her eyes and I could work in her deep waters to understand what was wrong. I asked God to help me understand what was the matter and to help me heal her and I had a vision: people who inspired my respect appeared before me, all well dressed in raw cotton like my father was when I ate mushrooms and had my first vision on the hillside, and I recognised my father Felisberto because he was the same as when I had seen him in my vision as a girl. When those people appeared I understood that they were the relatives I never knew, I understood that my grand-father was there, my great-grandfather, and all my other ancestors whose names I did not know, but I knew they were of my blood and I was of theirs and also that they were there to give me something. I knew I was the first woman to be in that place where they were and all the men before them had been, and that was why they were there, to give me something they knew was for me. Those men were not of flesh and bone, but I knew they had existed in another time, I knew they wanted to reveal something and that the mushroom Children had brought me to them for a reason that would soon be clear. When I approached them a table made of fine wood that smelled like the wet forest appeared, it smelled the way the forest smells after the rains with their fat drops refresh it, the table seemed like something from another world, as if the table were a sense of wellbeing and not a thing, and on the table appeared a book and just the sight of it gave me a beautiful feeling.

I didn't know happiness until I saw that book on the table. The book shone bright like the rays of sun shine into a dark and cold kitchen made of mud blocks and it's hard to look at them, the light is so strong and it shines on the many specks that float here and there, that was how I saw my ancestors through the shine of the Book, through that hot ray of sun, the blanket of specks and the ray of hot sun, and I saw my father Felisberto and my grandfather and my great-grandfather, and other men in my family I didn't know, I saw them just like I see you here in front of me, just like I see the interpreter there and it was a feeling, I had never been in such a pure and clean place, I'm not talking about the cleaning you do as a chore, I mean clean of body and the shine of your deep waters. It was like breathing the first air there ever was and the air cleaning all things deep down and I felt peace. Then three of them put their hands on the Book and the Book began to grow until it was the size of a child standing. I understood that I could open it and I did. There were letters on its pages, paragraphs I couldn't read but I did understand, because like I said to you, I never learned to read or write, my sister Francisca and I never knew studies, but this book was different from the ones they have in studies, it is the book of the Language and it is made of different materials, the pages were white and shone like light shines in the morning when the sun comes out of its mountain to take away the dark, this book had the power of heat. The cover was hot to the touch like a stone all day under the sun.

One of the beings I didn't know but who I knew belonged among my ancestors spoke and when I heard his voice I knew he was my great-grandfather. He was the one who said to me, Feliciana, this is the Book of the wise and it is for you, and the Book got smaller until it was the size of a church Bible, the ones that fit in your hand, and when I took it in my hand I realised that the shine wasn't something you only saw, it was something you felt in your whole body, it was heat and, most of all, it was the strength I was searching for. The beings and the wood table that smelled like the forest after a heavy rain disappeared and I was alone with the Book. And with the Book I felt stronger and less alone than ever before. I felt then that its strength was my strength, that was when I knew its strength was mine. I looked upon it and also upon my sister Francisca next to me with her eyes sunk into their hollows like black calabash cups and her breaths short and broken like a cracked mirror, my sister Francisca was breathing broken mirrors. I opened to the first page of the Book and could read the first lines to my sister Francisca, I began to sing because the lines were written like music and that was a gift given to me with each word because just saying each word created music. Before I went into my sister Francisca's deep waters to see what her sickness was, the

Children told me they were leading me by the hand of God because He is always the guide. The Children carry the wisdom that is the Language and the Language is in the Book.

I sang the first lines on the first page and when I finished the page I felt my heart full of strength, even more strength than when a pregnant woman feels the first kicks of a baby growing inside her because each word you say in the Language heals and healing is as powerful as giving life. I understood that all the curanderos in my family wanted to show me something but they couldn't guide me, the Language is what guides and teaches, that is its power. I understood that the first page was enough to heal my sister Francisca and so that is what I did until the sun came out of its mountain and when I stopped singing the words on that page of the Book it disappeared from my hands. That night my sister Francisca's sickness ended and I set out on the path of my name. That night when I healed my sister Francisca in the ceremony where I was given the Book, I realised that I owe the dead a greater debt than the living because the Language is theirs. Tell me, if the Language isn't power, then what is?

12

In their first session, a psychologist explained to Leandra that the act of talking about a loss moved the event, neurologically speaking, so it no longer carried the same weight. I once read an interview with Emil Cioran where he says that when he gets angry he curses nonstop until his rage is all used up. He says that he once wrote about suicide in his newspaper column; a woman found his number and called him to say that she was suffering terribly, that she was sick of being alive and wanted to know what had kept him from killing himself. He answered that if a person could still laugh, there was no reason for suicide. I read the interview at the office one day, and it hit me that Leandra had laughed that Saturday afternoon we spent together. A little less than before, but she'd laughed. She didn't talk about any of it directly, but she hadn't lost her sense of humour after my father died and the incident with that piece of shit Fernando. The fact that she was laughing but not talking about any of it seemed to me like symptoms at opposite extremes, like touching a hot surface with one hand and a cold one with the other to balance out daily life, knowing that if she took her hand away from either side, the other would freeze or burn.

Sometimes I wanted to ask her how she was, how she really was, but I also wanted to respect her process. I noticed she was laughing more often. Back then, Leandra was going to therapy once a week; my mother had good benefits at her job. She worked afternoons at the dentist's office, had a photography class on Saturdays, and was finishing high school. The next time we talked about it was after it had come up naturally in a conversation and Leandra had replied, without hesitating, It was unfortunate, Zo, but not as unfortunate as being that guy, being Fernando I mean. Imagine. That's really gotta be fucked up. The way she talked about him – and just the fact that she was talking about what had happened – made her seem stronger again. She was moving the memory. She started gaining back some of the weight she'd lost. One day, I noticed that her lips were almost red, without any lipstick, and her cheeks would flush when she was warm or laughing. One day, she put her hair up in a bun with little strands pulled free at her temples, and we chatted about nothing while she drank whole milk straight from the carton.

At the newspaper, I started spending more time with Julian, who was a year younger than me. I liked the gap between his front teeth; his hair was short and I was really into the single dreadlock that hung from the right side of his head. Sometimes he carried a skateboard in his back-pack, and he almost always wore a white cotton T-shirt. He wore one, once, that had a hole near the neck and I thought that was really sexy. A few weeks, or maybe a few months later, Julian invited me to a party. That was the first time I went out after my father died.

Julian was from Chihuahua. His mother left home when he was five and his father had raised him. His father was a maths professor at a university there and he couldn't leave his job, so he sent Julian to live with his uncle in Mexico City, in a small apartment with big windows that looked out over the avenue. The family had a little rooftop room they offered to their nephew.

Before I ever stepped foot inside, Julian told me that his uncle lived in a fifteen-bulb apartment and that his room had three: a light in the bathroom, a ceiling fixture in his room, and a little lamp. That was how he described his home to me. His room only had one window, in front of which he'd hung two square indigo-blue curtains with a white circular brushstroke in the middle of each, like the kind you'd see in a Japanese restaurant. He told me he'd bought them at a garage sale in Chihuahua. The bathroom had a thin wooden door with a brass knob that was more a suggestion than a door – you could hear everything. At first I was totally embarrassed by that, but soon we were getting along so well I forgot about it. The room smelled strongly of damp. He had a little cooker with two rings on a wooden shelf next to an industrial sink; he'd use it to boil water in a blue mug to make instant soups. Whenever his aunt passed him a container with food in it, he'd reheat us chicharrón en salsa verde, picadillo, or her speciality, meatballs stuffed with hardboiled egg and simmered in tomato sauce, or some kind of soup with pasta, and we'd eat. To give him opportunities he'd never had, so he could study whatever he wanted and work wherever he wanted, Julian's father scraped money together to pay Julian's uncle a symbolic sum to cover rent, so that Julian could pursue his art degree in the mornings and work with me in the afternoons at the newspaper, which he called the "snoozeroom".

It was early spring the first time I went to Julian's room. The heat was unbearable. He had a blue plastic cooler up there that sometimes had grape juice in it, the only kind he liked. He had a theory of romantic compatibility based on the favourite fruit of each person and how well they combined in juice form. That afternoon, we drank beer on the roof next to the water tank right across from his room. The paint on the building had faded and chipped over time, there were three distinct layers from the different colours the roof had been. A brownish one was the most prominent. I went into the bathroom and stared at the 100-watt Osram bulb. When I went back outside, I asked

Julian why he measured houses by light bulbs and he said that he'd been asked to count them once for the census. Now he counted them wherever he went; he knew, for example, how many there were at the newsroom. The sickest house I ever went to, he said once, had more than a hundred fucking light bulbs in it. What the fuck do you do with all those fucking lights? After that, I went home and counted the lights in our house. Most of them were soft white LED bulbs – my mother hates harsh light, she says daylight bulbs are for emergency rooms and make everyone look bad – that my father had switched us to one day to save energy and money, and then there were the red ones Leandra put in the garage when she set up her darkroom right next to where my father used to fix cars. The only bulbs I'd ever changed had been a tiny one in the refrigerator, and the one in the lamp next to my bed so I could keep reading after Leandra went to sleep without bothering her.

Even though it was perched above a busy avenue, the rooftop room where Julian lived felt isolated. You could hear more aeroplanes than noise from the street. That first time I went to his room, he showed me a guitar that his father had given him for his twelfth birthday. There were a few stickers on it, and someone had written the anarchy symbol with a Sharpie on the back. He also had a tattoo of a mathematical formula his father thought was especially beautiful. He showed me a few pencil drawings he'd done.

I'm not going to ask you to pose for me, all right? I just want to know what you think of them, he said to me with that northern accent I was falling hard for. He had a single mattress on the floor with a black bedspread, a passport-size photo of his mother when she was young, and another of his father as a little boy. I asked about them. He told me that his mother had gone to Piedras Negras and started another family. Her new husband didn't want any part of her past showing up in their present, so Julian and his father didn't have much communication with her; he had a brother who could barely speak Spanish and who he'd seen a couple of times – at a food court in the mall, give me a fucking break, he said. It had been his father who raised him.

Leandra had made a friend in her photography class, the two of them would go out together to take pictures. They also bought their film together, they were both vehemently against digital photography. The class was taught by a woman named Jacinta who usually wore only one earring, a long feather, and low-cut tank tops; she had big breasts and a big acrylic belt buckle with a scorpion inside it. When anyone asked her about it, she'd wax poetic about her zodiac sign, about how she also had Scorpio rising, and how the scorpion was her nahual, her spirit animal; the belt buckle served double duty as a button that jump-started a conversation about sun and rising signs. The first time I met her, I learned that Julian was a Cancer – which, she said, meant we were a perfect match. She hung her old-school Canon from a Huichol woven strap adorned with a Catholic trinket; that camera, with its enormous lens, was a goal for my sister. Jacinta wore her short hair parted in the middle. Leandra told me that she'd confessed in class one day that she didn't use soap to bathe, that she preferred to use a pre-Hispanic mix of fibres to wash her hair. My sister, who had made her own perfumes for a while already, had found herself a role model. Leandra became her favourite student; the teacher said she had lots of talent and was very smart. It was the first teacher in her entire life who had good things to say about Leandra, after all the schools that had kicked her out: one for misbehaving, another because of the giant hole she left when she threw a wet jacket over the ceiling fan, and another because of a fire she started in a garbage pail at school in defense of her friend Cuauhtémoc. Leandra's photography teacher told us that she was an excellent student – and used the same word to describe my sister's photos the first time Julian and I went to pick her up in the '78 Valiant. My mother was so thrilled that she invited Leandra out to dinner after her class just so she'd have a pretext for meeting her teacher.

Leandra told me she wanted to show her work in a gallery, even more than she wanted to be a designer. My father once said to me that he would have been a photographer if it had been up to him, but my grandfather was too uptight and, above all, too domineering. My father studied engineering and my uncle, accounting. His daughters, my cousins, grew up with the echo of that and ended up in law school. I have several memories of my father telling us in no uncertain terms that we could do whatever we wanted.

My father helped me put my drum kit together in the garage and Leandra knew that was the place for her darkroom, too. The garage was where he showed us that we had to work for it, sure, but there was always space for whatever we wanted to do. That was where I told him that I wanted to be a writer. Leandra learned to develop her photographs in the space where my father fixed blenders and toasters for our neighbours and my mother's co-workers, it was where he took whatever he could apart and put it back together. For all three of us, that garage was a space of freedom.

Leandra had started going out with boys at eleven, not long after Lalo broke her heart. She kissed a girl at a party when she was thirteen and had sex with a boy who lived on our street. She was always a step ahead of me in those things. At fourteen she hooked up with another girl; at fifteen she slept with one boy after another. Then with a girl. After the incident with that piece of shit Fernando, Leandra threw herself into her photography like I'd never seen her throw herself into anything besides hanging out with her friends. She'd become especially popular after the fire and got along well with the kids at the open education college where she ended up, everyone loved her at the dental practice where she worked, she was always cracking jokes. She got along with all different kinds of groups, you could drop her into any situation and she could have a conversation with anyone, and she hung out all over the place: sometimes I'd have to pick her up on the other end of the city – one of the conditions of the '78 Valiant was that I had to share it with my sister, but she didn't know how to drive and had no interest in learning. The friendship between her and the girl from her photography class kept growing.

Leandra was the receptionist at that dental practice for two years, until she turned eighteen. She liked her boss and was about to finish high school, and instead of the lost cause she'd seemed like before, she was the favourite in her photography class. By that age, Leandra had already been to three psychologists, the first when she was nine.

My mother, for her part, was spending more time with my aunt. She'd sometimes visit my other aunt, the wife of my father's brother, and she gradually returned to an active social life. It was hard for her to start going out again, but she began to make a routine of it, even while she kept some of the old routines she'd had with him: she still slept on the right side of the bed, and she still used the same chair at the kitchen table. No one ever took my father's seat. One time I noticed that she still carried in her purse the good luck charm he'd given her when they were dating. She was living in a house she rented with a bunch of students, including my uncle, who introduced them; in the living room, he'd given her a piece of pyrite in a little red felt bag. It was supposed to bring her luck in the entrance exam to study administration at the university. They told me that he'd helped her figure out some tricky maths problems, and that she'd made him laugh. I think that was always the nature of their relationship.

My sister's photography teacher thought she could include a few of the pictures from her class in a group show she was curating at the Centre for the Image. My sister felt honoured by the opportunity and was determined to be part of the show. She used to hate going to classes, they'd all seemed boring to her, until she discovered photography. I remember coming home drunk one night back then to find Leandra with plastic tongs in her hand and a crooked, messy top bun on her head, staring at different versions of the same image. She wanted to show them to me before I went to bed, but the red light made me feel sick and that time she was the one to help me to bed and tuck me in.

When she was thirteen, while she was still grounded for starting the fire and our parents were at work, my sister had sex with a neighbour she liked. The report was brief: His parents weren't home so I went over, he'd been playing soccer so he went to take a shower and I got in after him and then walked him dripping wet back to the bed. The story about Lalo in the pool with that girl in Tepoztlán had left such an impression on her that it was the first thing she did when she had a boyfriend. The report about the first girl she was with was similar: We were watching a film and I thought she looked beautiful in profile so I took her face in my hands and kissed her, and that led to something else, which led to something else. Leandra had always been comfortable and open about those things. I, on the other hand, had no idea how to approach a boy or a girl, though I knew I liked boys. The first time I worked up the nerve to try was with Julian. I was shy and nervous and clumsy, but I felt close to him and enjoyed his company. He made me feel safe. In retrospect, I think I got really lucky; our relationship helped me through a rough patch. I fell in love for the first time – and had sex for the first time – when I was nineteen years old and in my second year at university.

The first time we kissed, his hand trembled as he stroked my face and my mouth was dry from nerves. We were in his room, it was our second date. The connection between us was impossible to ignore and few days or maybe weeks later, before he left work he left a note on my work station one afternoon, a page torn out of a notebook with an invitation to spend the night with him written out in tiny letters. When I got back from the bathroom I nodded to let him know I would, and that was the first time we slept together. We set an alarm for 4:30am and he woke me up with his soft, gravelly voice. I got home just before dawn. Leandra and my mother were still asleep, and I managed to get a couple of hours in. The second time we did it was fun. I remember listening to a call-in show for people looking for romantic advice on his battery-powered radio, rolling around naked and cackling with laughter on his mattress right there on the floor.

The third time, I got pregnant. Technically, it shouldn't have happened, but it did. My period had been late before and I thought it was just happening again, between my job at the newspaper, which was pretty demanding, and my classes. I was three months late once in high school because of exam season, and when my father died I didn't get my period for two months. Even normal stress would sometimes push me back a couple of weeks, but this time I was two weeks late and something felt off. Still, I was sure there was no way I could be pregnant. We'd been fooling around and he'd penetrated me without a condom, but only for a second and then he'd put one right on, plus I was at a time in my cycle when it was really unlikely. Impossible, I thought. It never even crossed my mind, in fact, until I woke up tired one morning, even though I'd slept more than usual. A red light went on for me when I bought my favourite breakfast of a coffee and chocolate doughnut before class

and the smell turned my stomach. I couldn't eat the doughnut so I gave it to a classmate and drank the coffee. It tasted
horrible. That morning I'd run into my mother in the
kitchen and she'd asked me if I was all right. Maybe she'd
picked up on something even I wasn't aware of yet. I pulled
a tube of chapstick out of my backpack and that faint
strawberry smell was suddenly overpowering. I went to my
first class and spent the whole morning with nothing in
my stomach. After classes, on my way to work, I stopped
into a Sanborns. I was starving. I ate a bowl of chicken soup
alone in a four-person banquette and the nausea went away,
which confirmed my suspicions; all day I'd been feeling
like something was off, but I'd been doing everything I
could to ignore it. I bought a pregnancy test in the pharmacy section and brought it into the bathroom: positive.
I wandered around the store, not looking at anything in
particular – display cakes and magazine covers, everyone
in those pictures seemed so happy, smiling in uncomfortable positions, without a care besides looking cheerful. The
people working there, too, were calm in their routines, each
day was like the one before it; one was checking his phone,
another was leaning against a shelf with his arms crossed,
playing with his keyring, a young woman was ringing up a
cake. I stared at everything and saw nothing. The minutes
felt like days. I imagined all the possible outcomes of my
situation piling up in front of me until the pile collapsed

at my feet. I decided not to tell Julian over the phone. I went out to my car with the pregnancy test in my backpack. What was I going to do? I asked myself over and over in the car on the way to the newspaper. Whenever I had a negative thought, I'd see a kid in the car next to me and would wonder what it would be like to go through with it and whether the baby would look like my father, or Julian's mother, who he or she would probably never meet. I got tangled up in my questions like a giant spool of black yarn with the ends buried somewhere inside; trying to separate the strands only made it worse. It was hot and no open window in the world was going to give me enough air, no position was going to feel comfortable, no thought was going to calm me. Just as I was about to park near the newspaper, Leandra called me to say that her photography teacher had sent her an email to say that she'd chosen three of her pictures for the group show. My sister described the photos to me, I knew the ones but I couldn't concentrate on what she was saying; I heard that she wanted me to help her with the titles and told me a few she'd thought of, but it was like background music, I couldn't hear the words. I could tell, though, that she was happy. It had been a long time since I'd heard her like that. I felt a sense of peace for her, and at the same time I felt thunder, lightning, a whirlwind.

13

I healed my sister Francisca and whispers started to spread, the wind multiplied the whispers and someone came one night, someone else came another night and that was how people began to come for me to soothe their sick ones. This was before the foreigners started coming, when I healed my sister Francisca the whispers multiplied in the other towns, people came from the city and they said, I came from the city to see you, Feliciana. My name grew as the wind wished it and Paloma came to my house to tell me, Feliciana, honey, hold on, love, this is only the beginning, time to lose that grey face because you flash coloured lights. Paloma helped me with the relatives of the sick ones, she treated all of them well and the people who came to see me came to love Paloma right away.

My mother was dead by then, a few days before she died I found a bird dead on the ground and that was how my mother went, in her sleep as light as a bird flies she went and I couldn't do anything for her. My sister Francisca took over work in the milpa and in the kitchen, Aniceta made candles of pure beeswax that many people wanted, in the mornings she delivered them to the market and to a food store where for a few coins the woman who owned it made her a little space so she could sell her candles and other wares in the store, and that was how Aniceta began to bring our harvest there, and she could even put some of Apolonia's silks there inside in a case of wood and glass to show them off. Apolonia made the silk and cared for the worms and worked in the milpa, and Aparicio had started to help with the harvest, he wasn't in the pit next to the milpa anymore even though I left the pit there because I didn't know when I might need to throw him back in it, but from one day to the next the boy made himself useful, he stopped crying there in the pit and that was when I took him out because he was making a serious face that reminded me of my father Felisberto who even took his sweet coffee in the morning with a serious face. My father was a serious man just like my son Aparicio has always been serious, he never laughed the way other children laugh and because of this Paloma came to my house one day to say to me, Feliciana, my darling, that son of yours went from being a baby to being a respectable old man, here, I brought you these tiny boots for the little man of the house, I hope he doesn't scold me for forgetting his hat and his cattle.

We collected our coins between all of us, and all of us ate the cornmeal and beans and chayote and chiles and coffee that my sister Francisca made. More and more people came to see me for ceremonies, and coins came into our home that way as well. Paloma helped me prepare my ceremonies, she taught Apolonia to put on make-up so she could go out sparkling in the mornings, she taught Aparicio to treat his sisters well because he had a dark side that was Nicanor's dark side when he was drunk, but Aparicio had it already as a child, without even reaching the age for liquor he already had Nicanor's dark side and my father Felisberto's serious face. Paloma said to me, Feliciana, the boots don't make the macho, love, Nicanor had a bad temper because he was a bad seed, but I said to her No, Nicanor wasn't a bad seed, it was the war and the liquor that made him like that, and Paloma said to me, Feliciana, bring Aparicio to me, I'll take him to the market or to town or wherever but I'll take him with me so he knows how to get along with other people because that pit raised him wrong, children learn in the street, at least you didn't put a mirror down in that pit with him or he'd be just impossible now, there's still hope, love, leave him with me and I'll introduce him to the street and we'll pull him out of that pit.

The second time death called to Paloma was when she loved a man she met when she took Aparicio into town, a loveless man whose mother was beaten to death and who knew no affection from men or women. Paloma met him with Aparicio, the man asked her about the boy's boots to have something to say and Paloma understood it was a request for nights, she arranged to see him that night, but he had been a loveless man since he came into this world and knew nothing about how to treat men or women, and the night was just as loveless when death laid its egg in Paloma for the second time, when it trilled its song to her, I know it was that loveless man who spat in her face and opened the scar on her brow that she had from the beating she got for the way she walked, like she had feathers said my grandfather Cosme, and that loveless man beat Paloma's face open again.

They say that if a person runs into shadows it is because they bring light, and that was how it was for Paloma, her mouth was purple from the beating that loveless man gave her, and with her mouth still purple from the beating she got from his lovelessness she met José Guadalupe, the man she lived with and the one who found her with the stain of blood growing bigger under her when they killed her with a knife in her back, Paloma met her love the time when they beat her face open again, opening her brow that had already been opened like a mirror of lovelessness, that was when she met Guadalupe when I was healing the people who came to me sick, and when my name travelled through the towns and from there to other towns and the whisper grew and spread to the city and from there to other cities, which is why I say that the wind multiplies, because though we fear the wind when it takes our harvest and we fear the wind when it brings hail that ruins our harvest, I say don't fear the storm because the wind multiplies and when the storms come with their hail listen to the sound they make when the hail falls like icy knives and listen to the storm, you have to listen to the sky's thundering because it is no secret that the wind multiplies, and so I say to you trust it, this is also part of life because the wind multiplies. It multiplies good fortune also.

One day Mr Tarsone came to San Felipe to find me, he arrived asking for me by my name, he arrived asking for me because he had watched me in that film, the whispers reached him and that's how the gringo banker arrived who brought the people who grew my name. Paloma knew that my name was growing, that people came here asking for me and she said to me, Feliciana, darling, look at you, love, you're famous now but you're not celebrating like a famous person, here's what we'll do, you get good and famous so I can celebrate like a famous person, with plenty of liquor and love. And Paloma and I spent a few nights smoking cigarettes and drinking liquor and laughing together while the others slept.

One-eyed Tadeo appeared when he heard the noises of people coming and the noises of coins dropping. I told the people who came that I don't see the future, I offer myself to God in prayer every day and every night and in what I do there is no hate or rage or lies. I don't see the future, I see the present through the Language, I am no fortune-teller and that was how One-eyed Tadeo was tricking people, with the clairvoyances he told people he was seeing with his bad eye. He took advantage of that eye, he told people he saw the future with his bad eye and they believed him. But I don't pay attention if people come tell me to tell them the future, I tell them that I clean like the water cleans, I clean the sicknesses of the body, I clean people's deep waters like water that flows and smooths the stones of the river with its flowing, I clean sicknesses of the body like water cleans dirt from the body and heaviness from the gut, I clean the shadows which are sufferings because light exists but darkness is its brood. I am no magician, it is the Language that heals, but there are people who are distressed by the future and that is what clairvoyances are for, and there are people who believe that sickness can only be cured with the medicines in pills and elixirs made in laboratories by men in white coats and that's what the sages of medicine prescribe, but sickness comes in many forms and not all sicknesses can be cured with medicines from a laboratory, everyone knows that there are more sicknesses than pills and if all the sicknesses of the body and the soul could be cured by pills, imagine, the world would be new with health as if every morning was the first morning of the world, the first morning of God.

One-eyed Tadeo lives on the other side of the gully and the mist, on the other side of San Felipe, he almost never leaves his hut because of his bad eye, they say it got that way when someone broke a bottle of liquor over his head and then crushed it into his eye, I knew him when he was a little boy and he looked at me with both eyes, before he had that black calabash cup where his eye used to be, when we left San Juan de los Lagos to live in San Felipe, Tadeo saw with both eyes and said he saw things in his dreams. Every town has its brujo and Tadeo wanted to be the town brujo since he was a boy, every town has its brujo and there are even brujos inside those devices the foreigners bring. One-eyed Tadeo called out to people, he said, Feliciana will give you mushrooms and herbs that will make you vomit, those mushrooms and herbs that she gives, but I can tell your future without giving you anything that will make you sick. And he would throw his seven kernels of corn, he would throw cards and he would say that the cards and the corn spoke to him with their strength, that seven powers spoke to him, and if someone came to him with a sickness he would give them a mix of herbs and cooking oil for them to take, and Paloma would say, Feliciana, he's so big and fat, love, God made him big and fat like a maraca, darling, to hold all those kernels of corn, because he's hollow inside, there's nothing there just like there's nothing where his eye used to be.

One-eyed Tadeo made people believe that the future spoke through his cards and his kernels of corn. Paloma said to me once, Feliciana, love, you're not going to believe this but the Maraca is going around saying that he saw a storm with his bad eye, that a hail storm is coming to destroy the harvest, and he the bad seed went out to throw kernels of corn at the sky, he started yelling at the sky to make the hail fall somewhere else, he yelled at the thunder to make it fall somewhere else and he yelled so loud everyone got scared about what the Maraca was yelling at the sky. And then later people said the hail didn't fall because of what One-eyed Tadeo yelled at the sky like the bad seed he is. One-eyed Tadeo is dead now, the liquor drowned him, he was the one who shot me in the shoulder with a pistol a long time ago, when Mr Tarsone made all the people come to see me, One-eyed Tadeo hated that and was jealous of the coins that came. He never talked much, no, One-eyed Tadeo never talked much, his teeth were smaller than his gums and his words were smaller than his head, and people went see him as more people came looking for me because he said he could see the future with his bad eye and because he never talked much he seemed wise and when he told people the future he told them the future to fit the person in front of him, the Language is also like a poncho that can fit anyone when it is used to tell the future, and with his bad eye he told the girls who wanted to know if a boy liked them that yes, the boy was on his way to tell her, the cards were bringing him to her, and he told the wives their husbands were not faithful and he purified them all with the same herbs and with some of them he went far, he grabbed the girls when he was purifying them, when he moved the candles and the eggs over them he also touched their breasts and more, but then to other girls he said your husband is faithful and he threw his kernels of corn and said look, the kernels of corn say your husband is faithful, and those girls he didn't touch. Paloma used to laugh at him, she called him the Maraca, because she was a curandera by blood, and even though she had turned her back on healing for parties and for nights with men and for life with Guadalupe it angered her that One-eyed Tadeo took advantage of people.

Paloma was angry once with Apolonia because she went to see One-eyed Tadeo. Selling silk from house to house, she had met a boy and felt attracted to him but he did not share her feeling and she went to One-eyed Tadeo who threw his seven kernels of corn and threw his cards and gave her a mix of herbs and cooking oil and charged her what she had saved from what she brought for expenses, and he also asked her for a bottle of liquor that Apolonia went to buy from Aniceta at the store. When Apolonia brought One-eyed Tadeo the bottle of liquor he told her that the boy who did not have the same feeling for her would go to her house and ask for her in marriage with a bride price for me, her mother, and that the cards told him to purify her path with herbs and cooking oil so the boy would go to her house, he told her that they would have two children right away, even three children he saw in her future, he said, and Apolonia went away happy because the boy was going to share her feeling, because he was going to ask for her in marriage, because he was ready with the bride price and they were going to have children soon, maybe even three. Apolonia fed the mulberry leaves to the silkworms and she filled them almost to bursting with her thoughts about the names she liked of our dead relatives and the names of people she sold her silk to so that when her children with this boy who didn't share her feeling arrived she could tell him the names she liked, but soon after that a girl pregnant with the boy's child came into the store and Aniceta told Apolonia that the boy she liked had a wife and she was pregnant. Apolonia broke into pieces and I couldn't say to her, Why did you go see him, child, they tell you the pot will burn you and you grab it with both hands, no, I couldn't say that, I asked her to go with me to the milpa and I talked about the rains that would come, of the heat, of nature's cycles, because if those cycles are broken then the seasons change because time doesn't move in a line, time moves in a circle. I don't know if my daughter Apolonia understood what I meant, but no one else can teach us the lessons we learn in life and so I talked to her about nature, because nature has the answers to the ills we suffer, you just have to watch the circles time moves in to understand our nature, the nature of people.

So I tell you, I don't see the future and I can't stop a person from dying if death has laid its egg in them and that is the will of God, I can't do anything about that, but if someone comes to me sick and they can be healed, I heal them because that is to lift someone up who has fallen along the path, people need help to keep moving forward, and lifting us up when we fall is something the Language does. The sages of medicine see people in pieces, an ear, a foot, a hand, arthritis, the sages of medicine only see the pieces of people because that's what they learned in their studies, but you have to see the whole of a person who is sick if you want to understand their illness because everything is connected, the body is one, and that is a thing the Language does. I saw that the Language could cure sickness buried in the soul when Paloma brought Guadalupe to me. Here in San Felipe life is hard for Muxes because they are not allowed to be in a couple, forget about marriage, that doesn't happen here in San Felipe because Muxes are born to care for their family, but Paloma's mother was dead, her father Gaspar was also dead, she never met him because he died while her mother was pregnant, so she didn't have any family to take care of when she became Muxe. We were her family, me and my children. There are people who look down on Muxes but most people in San Felipe respect them, many accept their kindnesses but in return they give more thorns than roses, if they give roses at all. Paloma knew everyone and everyone loved her. She had Guadalupe and she could live with him because she didn't have family to take care of, she also had friends she could go out with, but Guadalupe fell sick just after he went to live with Paloma.

Paloma and two of her friends carried Guadalupe to me after he faded. They told me he hit his head when he fell and he had convulsions, and that he fell again from their arms when they carried him. I saw right away that it was serious, but his sickness wasn't physical, instead he had a sickness buried in his soul because he had been humiliated and abused, and the sickness came when he went to live with Paloma, Guadalupe had his father buried inside him, his father who humiliated and was cruel to him, I'd seen the man in town and he was cruel to Guadalupe and laughed at him, and Guadalupe carried that man around rotting his soul from the inside, but I couldn't tell Paloma that, even though she is my blood I must not say what I see, that belongs to God, and Guadalupe needed to tell her the sickness buried inside him because that is the Language, also, to shine light in the darkness. Not to see people in little pieces but to see the whole person, because the body is one.

I don't need a sick person to tell me what is wrong, I can see it. A sick person can guide me the same way the sages of medicine ask their sick ones questions but they don't need to tell me what's wrong, that I can see with the Language. I only need to know their name and I can get inside. But I can only work with people who speak because what was given to me was the Language. Once a man came to me who had no voice, a mute man came to see me, and another time a girl came to see me who had no voice, it had been lost to her. Both of them were very sick with other sufferings but just like they came they had to go to another town and see a curandero there because I could not help them. They once brought me a little girl with the sickness of silence, she knew how to talk but she refused to talk and she made waters when they yelled at her and hit her to make her talk, and when I asked the girl her name I could see and feel that the girl had been abused by some wretch but I couldn't see him, she didn't let me in, and if she didn't talk to me I couldn't help her so I gave her my blessing and told her mother to take her to a sage of medicine because her daughter was sick but not because she wet herself, she was sick with the silence of shame and she wet herself because of guilt, because of fear, just like my sister Francisca did but I couldn't tell her more, I only said she should take her daughter to a sage of medicine because she was wetting herself for a reason that was not the sickness of silence.

There are people who fear us because they don't understand what we do. I am not a witch or a fortune-teller or a healer like the others, God knows that, the herbs and the mushrooms give me great powers for reflection because that is the greatest power we have on this earth, reflection is how we heal ourselves and how we can fix any problem or heartbreak, and so with herbs and with the mushroom Children I look inside the sick one, I see the root of their physical sickness or the suffering buried in their soul and that is something the sages of medicine can't do, people are afraid of us because they don't know how we do it, but this is something that comes to us from our ancestors, it is as old as the land itself.

After the ceremony for my sister Francisca I knew I could heal anyone of any suffering no matter the shadows around it, but it was with Guadalupe that I saw I could heal sufferings buried deep in the soul, that was another thing Paloma taught me when she carried Guadalupe to me. That's why I said to you that you have the Language, Zoe, people who use the Language to help people see things also have it, even if they don't make ceremonies.

People say to me, Feliciana, how can you be the shaman of the Language if you don't speak the same tongue as the people you heal, and I say to them, I'm not the shaman of the kinds of languages people speak, there are machines for that, I have the Language and it lets me see yours and that is a different thing. Before my initiation I didn't know many of the words I use now, this is something that happens with the Language, you use a word you don't know and when you say it you understand what it means because God is the Language and when you say the words you are also creating a world, another world like this one but not the same.

Sickness does not distinguish between people, professions or social classes. A newborn gets as sick from the same suffering as an elder, a boy rich in coins and a poor one get sick just the same, a wretch and a good man, an unlucky girl and a fortunate one. It has been this way since the time of our ancestors, but the advances of medicine do not yet reach all the corners where wisdom reaches. That is the difference between a sage and a scientist, the sage can see everything through reflection, but the scientist is limited to what he knows. The Language is nature, the Language is in the herbs and in the mushroom Children that allow us to reflect, there is no corner the mushroom Children and sacred herbs made by the hand of God can't reach with their games, and this is how I heal with my hands those things that certain doctors are not able to heal, what the mushroom Children allow me to see isn't the future of fortune-tellers or the past where resentments lie, they let me see the present which is as vast and unknown as the body, the body we all have but none of us really knows, this was what I saw when I healed Paloma's love Guadalupe in the ceremony when she brought him to me sick with convulsions.

Paloma and Guadalupe and two of Paloma's friends were drinking pulque and liquor when Guadalupe faded and fell off his chair. From high up he fell. They thought he had faded because he hadn't eaten, Paloma said he hadn't eaten even a tortilla for breakfast, he'd taken a cup of black coffee but that was all. They tried to revive him, they splashed him with water, rubbed him with alcohol. A whisper went out and soon two more friends arrived and they took Guadalupe outside so the air could refresh him but he did not revive. One of her friends gave him a black syrup and that was when Guadalupe began his convulsions. Paloma and her two friends came terrified to my door, Paloma was white like the moon and her eyes were just as distant, sweating and frightened she told me what had happened and helped me prepare the ceremony, they knew he was very sick but they didn't know with what. Paloma said to me, Feliciana, he's like a bull, darling, help him, love, because if he goes my heart goes with him, love, heal him like I healed your grandmother Paz or my heart goes with him, darling, heal him like your grandfather healed my father, heal him like you healed Francisca because now you're the only one who can, you have the Language and the Book is yours. When they left, I passed a candle over Guadalupe to look at him well and the candle told me with its flame that Guadalupe was ill but there was not a single wound from the times they told me he fell, there was not a single mark on his body from what had happened and then he had a convulsion right there. That was when the flame told me the path to his healing.

I passed my hands over him and his convulsion passed, I asked for his name and was able to go inside. Guadalupe as a little boy is walking in a tunic of orange cloth, a flame orange like a fire at night that catches people's eyes in the street, and in his walking he is serious, like an adult with a past that weighs on him, and he walks like that toward his father who is across the street in clothes made of rough cloth. His father looks at him in his flame orange tunic and laughs, he says, You're dressed like those old spinsters not even a dog or flies will go near, and in that moment someone shoots his father with a rifle and his father falls. Young Guadalupe in his tunic like orange flames in the night sees the blood begin to stain his father's rough cloth and runs to help him when the same rifle shoots at the little boy dressed in orange like flames in the night, only it doesn't hit him, it hits the father who is wounded and wounds him more, and that is how I understood it was the spirit of the boy that was wounded and not his body, and that it was his father who made the wound in his soul. I saw that his father's wounds from the bullets were very serious, that the boy had not been hit and that it caused him great guilt, and he faded because of it, to compensate, and I saw that he had gotten sick many times before he met Paloma, to compensate, and I saw these sufferings very quickly, but in that moment like in all the other moments the boy dressed in orange like a flame in the night was searching for death to be on the same level as his father, the boy loved his father. I went over to the two of them before the father died and I told the boy that his father was going to die anyway, that it wasn't his fault, that if they shot one more time they would have hit him, too. I sang him a page from the Book so he could settle things with his father and heal the sickness in his deep waters. The boy dressed in orange spoke with his father and when the sun came out I went out to Paloma, and I saw the anguish in her face and her makeup all streaked, I saw that she hadn't slept, the other two Muxes who came with her were gone and I told her that Guadalupe would be better after seven days and seven nights, and that after forty days and forty nights he would be happy. After the new moon Guadalupe came to give me a few coins and he brought me breakfast.

No, I don't charge for my service, someone like me doesn't charge for what they do. Politicians charge, liars charge and fools charge double as my grandfather Cosme always used to say, but you can't put a price in coins on knowledge, and knowing something is the same as seeing and you don't take money for telling someone what you see, especially not in the service of God. People bring me coins for what I do and I have coins from all over the world, I receive with gratitude what the people who seek my services offer me but I don't sell. I am just as grateful for a cup of sweet coffee, just like my father Felisberto liked to take it, my father with his serious face, just like my son Aparicio was always serious as a little boy, just like Guadalupe and I drank our sweet coffee when he came to see me after he recovered, and I also am grateful to whoever gives me coins because at home we've always been many mouths to feed.

A few months after Guadalupe got better, Paloma came to tell me, Feliciana, love, Guadalupe is feeling good as new and look, sweetheart, he sends you these flowers he cut himself on the hillside. And do you know what flowers he sent me? A bouquet of bright orange flowers, orange like a flame in the night, orange like the tunic he was wearing as a boy in my vision. I spoke with him when the sun came out of its mountain and he didn't remember the ceremony or how he was dressed in the vision or how serious he looked at the market, and he never said anything about his father's cruelty, because sometimes I see one thing and what the sick person sees is something else, the Language is like that, if I say Tree I see a tree and you see a different tree, but things are more connected than what we see with our eyes, that is what the present shows, that is what I see. Even though you see one tree and I see another, they are connected in their deep waters, and that is the Language. I never told Guadalupe the colour of his tunic, I never told him about the vision I had in his deep waters when he came to see me for breakfast. When Paloma gave me the flowers he had cut to thank me because he was happy I knew the page of the Book they were coming from as if Guadalupe had sent me the flowers straight from his deep waters, as if Guadalupe the boy had brought flowers to the war with his father, because people bring flowers to their battlefields just like Paloma said when she marked the scar on her brow so it would stand out, and when I saw the flowers he sent me with Paloma I was happy to know his soul was well and that Guadalupe the man was also bringing flowers to Guadalupe the boy, and that the flame orange like a fire in the night that was once the cruelty of his father who humiliated him so many times had been transformed into a bouquet.

14

I got an abortion when it was still illegal in Mexico City. I had tried first with a pill, but it hadn't worked. I didn't tell my sister or my mother, either, but I knew she suspected something. We went to a building in the Zona Rosa, I remember it was on the seventh floor and it had an amazing view of the city. A friend from the university had told me to knock on the only white door on that floor, but not to ring the bell. A woman let us in, then had us wait in a room with old magazines in it and a television with the volume turned all the way up. The form she gave me didn't ask for any of Julian's personal information. An impulse I can't explain made me fill out the form as if I were my sister, and I showed it to Julian so he'd know to call me Leandra. He nodded, then went down to the 7-Eleven across the street. There were questions on the form about how many sexual partners I'd had, what religion I was, what drugs I took and how often, and at the end there was a paragraph detailing what could happen to me if something went wrong, a few potential causes of death, and a statement that indicated that by signing I promised not to hold the doctor at the clinic responsible. Julian came back with two Cokes. I didn't drink mine right then because they were going to give me anaesthesia. No liquids was one of the few instructions I'd received when I made the appointment over the phone.

How did you hear about us, asked the woman who gave me the form and collected it. She had short, highlighted hair and elaborate nails, before acrylics were in style. A friend. Alright, she said curtly, put on that robe, the doctor's ready to see you. On my way to the bathroom I passed several closed doors and one that was a little bit ajar; inside, a girl was asleep on a cot. On the other side of the room was an open door with a metal operating table behind it, a surgeon's lamp and a small rectangular window with vertical blinds. The apartment had parquet flooring, and the walls and ceiling were stuccoed. There were white circles around the energy-saving lightbulbs where ceiling fixtures had once been, and pale squares on the walls where photos and paintings used to hang. Together, these ghostly geometries were evidence that the place was a rental and had probably been home to a family before. I came back from the bathroom and noticed that the woman with the acrylic nails had the Chanel logo painted on them by hand. They weren't all identical, but each nail had a miniscule rhinestone where the backs of the two Cs met. Julian took the money we'd scraped together out of his backpack and she counted the stack of small bills twice; my clearest memory is that she had her desk lamp on in the middle of the day and her nails sparkled under its light.

The doctor I'd spoken with over the phone explained the procedure to me on the back of a prescription pad with drawings that were little more than stray lines and circles. I was in the ninth week and he was going to perform an aspiration, which he described as straightforward. I didn't feel comfortable there, but I'd been lucky: I trusted the doctor. The first thing I thought was that I could stop worrying, at least, about that terrifying last paragraph on the form. He asked me what I was studying and where I worked, told me that I wouldn't be charged for two check-ups I'd need after the procedure, and said he expected me to return to classes and the newsroom as soon as I felt up to it.

An anaesthetist with limp eyelashes, droopy brows, no make-up and short cropped hair, who gave off nun vibes and smelled strongly of lotion (it's the only smell I remember from that day and the scent brings me back every time I've come across it since then), and who ironically referred to me as "the mother", asked me to count backwards from 100. I only got through about four numbers before I was out cold. When I came to, the woman with the Chanel logo on her nails said, We're all done, rest a little and then you can go home. I asked her about Julian, she told me that he hadn't moved from the waiting room and that we'd be able to leave soon. I fell asleep for a bit, but I was woken up by a horrible cramp and, through a curtain of painkillers that seemed to go transparent right before my eyes, I got to my feet. Julian ran over to me as soon as I reached the door, and just before we got to the waiting room the woman with the Chanel nails said to me, I know it hurts, and it's going to hurt for another three or four days, but when you leave the building try to stand up straight, sweetheart, especially in the elevator – no whimpering or grabbing your belly please, because of the neighbours.

We'd taken the metro to the clinic but we went back to Julian's room in a taxi. It felt like we had to climb a thousand stairs to get to the roof. I was in more pain than when we'd left. I got into his bed and fell asleep at 1.30 in the afternoon; we slept together there in his bed on the floor, and when I woke up it was already night and apparently it had rained but I hadn't noticed at all. I hadn't expected Julian to be affected, but things hit us unexpectedly sometimes, the way one ball sometimes hits another unexpectedly in a game of pool, and he lit a candle and stuck it in an empty bottle of wine we'd picked up at the corner store. Avoiding my eyes, he asked my forgiveness for not being ready for fatherhood. I found it unsettling – I'd never suggested that, not even as a possibility. He told me about one weekend he spent waiting for a call from his mother in Piedras Negras, and the call never came. She'd left him in his father's care, and what he and I had just been through made him feel guilty, like he was becoming everything that had hurt him when he was young. I didn't feel guilt or sadness, really. What I felt was a lot of physical pain. The first few hours, I realised later, were the worst. Julian had saved the Coca Cola I hadn't been able to drink before, and that was the only thing I ingested that day. I fell back asleep and slept until Leandra's phone call woke me up the next day.

I'd left the Valiant at home. My sister thought I was at a friend's house and wanted to ask me if she could use it, with someone else driving, of course, and whether I'd be home for dinner. Julian had gone to the library, and while I was on the phone with my sister I read his note telling me he'd be back soon. It was Saturday, I didn't have to go to work and could stay in bed all day if I wanted. As I listened to my sister's voice without managing to focus on her words, I remembered my dream from the night before: I was inside an unfamiliar house that seemed perfectly normal, but then when I went outside I noticed I could see through the walls. I went back inside the house, which belonged to someone else. I don't know who and I don't know why I was there alone. I noticed that the walls were turning transparent right before my eyes and that the roof was made of glass. I thought no one would see me because no one was around, but suddenly three teenagers I didn't know passed by and looked inside. They pointed at me and one of them laughed. There was a sprinkler in the garden and I felt calm looking through the streams of water. A dog appeared and started playing with the sprinkler, and I realised that I wasn't as alone out there as I was inside the transparent house. The dog seemed like good company; actually, the best. I didn't go back inside the transparent house and the dog began to follow me as I strolled aimlessly. While Leandra was telling me about who was planning to attend the group show – apparently a bunch of artists, gallerists, and editors Jacinta knew, plus friends of friends of my sister's – I suddenly understood that I'd given her name at the clinic as a way to hide from a situation that made me feel bad. I wasn't comfortable inside the house in my dream because the walls were transparent, and with my sister's voice as a backdrop, I realised that it was better to be outside than living inside a farce. There's nowhere to hide, especially not when it comes to something like this. Anyway, I didn't want to hide, and even though I couldn't focus on what Leandra was saying, it meant everything to hear her voice. Why had I hidden behind my sister's name? Why hadn't I said anything? Was I ashamed? Why should I have to justify anything? I went home that night, after falling asleep again and waking up hungry. On Monday I went back to my classes, and on my way to work I called two animal shelters. A few days later, I came home with a dog. My period was late after the induced bleed but it returned to normal before long. My mother hadn't gotten home from work yet when Leandra saw the dog. I explained to her in detail the different options I'd considered at the shelter and while I described another dog I'd liked, Leandra started calling the one I'd brought home Rumba because of the way she lurched across the slippery floor in our freshly mopped kitchen. I told Leandra I'd had an abortion a few days earlier. You should have told me, sis, she said. I would've gone with you.

Years passed and I have no regrets; in fact, I'd do it all again today. Julian quickly got over his guilt. We haven't spoken in a long time; we lost touch in part because he went to live with his father in Chihuahua, and in part because that's just how the cards fell. Not long after my thirty-third birthday, someone at the newspaper ordered food from a nearby restaurant and a kid around fourteen, fifteen years old showed up carrying a brown tray with melamine plates, glasses, and cups of yellow pudding, which he distributed among those of us ordered. Something about his movements reminded me of Julian, and that was the only time I thought about the fact that if I had given birth to a boy at nineteen, he'd have been the same age by then and would probably move like the kid who brought us our food. The longer I watched him, the more convinced I was that the son I never had with Julian would have been just like him.

I always thought that all you had to do to get pregnant was stop being careful for three months at most and you'd be holding a positive test, but that's not how it happened with Felix. I spent so long being so careful to prevent it from happening again that it never occurred to me that it might take years of trying. I talked about it with my mother a few times, and she always cut the conversation short by saying, You can tug on the flower, Zoe, but it won't grow any quicker. My mother has five or six generic phrases that my father, Leandra and I knew all too well, and which she used to close up shop on all kinds of discussions. During those years when Manuel and I stopped taking precautions and I didn't know whether it would happen or not, that line about the flower marked the end of the conversation. I asked her a few times to use her clairvoyance to tell me if we were going to get pregnant or not, especially when I started wondering if it was even possible. I didn't want medical advice from her, I just wanted her to tell me everything was going to be all right, but she'd close her eyes, tell me to give her a minute to connect with the other side, and then deliver that same line about the stupid flower. Then she'd laugh at the expression on my face and say, It's time you learned that life isn't like consumer culture, Zoe, it's not on demand. Anyway, there's no such thing as oracles, things happen when the moment is right.

This was the same person who greeted me at the door

one day when I went to visit her with, Well, well, look at you! Pregnancy suits you. It was too early for any test to detect the pregnancy and I didn't feel different or strange at all. It was unlikely that month, anyway, since the two of us had been working a lot, but a couple of weeks later I called to tell her about those two pink lines and she calmly replied, Yes, Zoe, I know. A healthy, adorable baby boy. Your father must be so happy, wherever he is, to know his first grandchild is on the way.

Manuel and I were thrilled. I remember him going online that night to look for pushchairs, and how sweet I'd thought that was, but I have no idea how my mother was so sure that Felix was going to be Felix, whether it was intuition, a lucky guess, or who the hell knows.

Leandra started dating a girl around the same time she was in her photography class. Anna was the younger sister of the dentist Leandra worked for; they'd seen each other a couple of times in the dentist's office and then ran into each other at a party, and that's how they started dating. Anna was a few years older than us. She was a vet and was doing a residency treating the horses at a riding club to finish her degree. She had a pompadour that she dyed blue and wore to one side; her black hair was almost always tied back in a short ponytail. Whenever you looked her in the eye, she'd push her thick-framed glasses up the bridge of her nose, even if they hadn't slipped down, as if she felt exposed. She had broad shoulders and her arms were marked by hives and a big, round scar from a vaccine. She was quick to blush and had a deep voice like Leandra did back then, but even deeper, and she talked slowly. Leandra's voice had filled out and her laughter was contagious, they filled the space wherever she went. At seventeen she'd walk back to our room naked from the bathroom; she was comfortable in her body, and her laughter reflected that comfort. When she was thirteen, around the same time she started that fire, my sister would say audacious things, but she'd say them quietly. Over time she gained confidence, like someone who starts out with small handwriting and then later starts to write in big, looping letters, ignoring the lines on the page. In my role as big sister I remember trying to help Leandra a few times when I thought she needed it, like when my father asked her to get a few pieces he needed for a car he was working on and I thought she wouldn't be able to carry them alone; my father popped out from under the car to tell me, Don't help her, Zoe, Lea can handle anything. That kind of comment gave her a solid foundation, and probably made her more confident. By the time she was seventeen I think Leandra had gotten over the need for attention she had at thirteen, she was more secure in who she was.

Her girlfriend Anna was the complete opposite. It was like she was ashamed of her material presence, like she was trying to erase herself with her long pauses and her low voice, which made it hard to follow what she was saying; listening to her was like trying to read words written without pressing the pencil into the paper. One Saturday, Leandra called my cell phone to say that Anna had gotten a tattoo on her arm and that she was going to get one soon, too. Julian and I went to the cinema with them that afternoon; below her round vaccination scar, Anna's tattoo was covered with gauze and a plastic film, so we couldn't see it. They had one party to go to and we had another, but before we parted ways, we went for dinner together. I was able to see the dynamic between Anna and my sister up close. It was clear to me that Leandra wasn't sure of anything the future might hold, but she was sure of herself and that seemed to attract Anna, who seemed sure of everything but herself. My sister made some comment about sex and Anna got angry with her. Leandra gave Anna a kiss, which scandalised a Respectable Lady who was feeding soup to a young child at the next table over, and Leandra said she was going to give the scandalised woman a kiss on the way to the bathroom to help her get over the shock. I followed her to the bathroom. After washing her hands she dried them by running her fingers through her hair, like she always did back then. Two for one, sis, she said, you dry your hands and fix your hair in one go. She usually left the bathroom with her long fringe pushed to one side, and while she was styling it she asked me what I'd thought of Anna. We hadn't spoken much, but I liked her. I asked Leandra if she was happy and, as she retouched her lipstick with a tube she carried in her trouser pocket, she said, Fuck that lady, and fuck all those judgmental pieces of shit out there. If they had any idea how good kissing your girlfriend feels, but no, they have to pull a fucking face whenever anyone does anything they don't agree with. What do you think of her tattoo? she asked, showing me the drawing on her phone: it was the face of a little dog, a cartoon she'd found on the internet. I wanted to do the drawing for her in three or four simple lines, but I like how it turned out, Leandra had said. It wasn't long before she got her first tattoo, though she kept the promise she'd made to my father.

With her fingers, Leandra showed me where on her arm her first tattoo was going to go and walked in front of me back to the table.

"You should get one, too, sis. Better to stand out in a morgue for some terrible tattoo that you regret, like a fucking Bugs Bunny that's so fucked up it looks like a roast chicken, but at least no one else has the same ink, and I say that in the morgue, where we're all equal, it must be pretty cool for someone to be like, hey, check this out, this one has a fucking roast chicken on her arm, and someone else to be like, I love roast chicken and avocado sandwiches, man, and then the two of them go on and on about roast chickens because of your fucked up Bugs Bunny tattoo, but at least you stand out from the others and you've given them something to talk about."

Leandra took Anna to the opening of her group show at the Centre for the Image. One of the other photographers in the show flirted with Leandra. We found out later that he was thirty-one, which seemed really old at the time. Julian and I speculated about his personal life, and why he was flirting with Leandra, who had until just recently been a minor. All it took was that brief exchange for Anna to throw a fit. She and Leandra argued on a street corner, and I remember my sister's smile as she switched her parting from one side to the other, that wavy hair she'd inherited from my father, while Anna pushed her glasses up her nose; her tic was out of control. From where I stood, it was clear that Leandra wasn't about to get sucked into the jealous scene Anna was making, in fact, she had no interest in anything that wasn't the opening. She was happy to be there, and she was clearly not going to let anyone rain on her parade. Anna stormed off to the bathroom and we didn't see her for the rest of the night. That show marked the beginning of my sister's career, it was an important day for her. Maybe we all have a day like that when we're teenagers, a day that invites us to our future, sometimes in the form of a comment made by someone older that determines our path.

That night a man approached Leandra about publishing one of her photos in a magazine and a short blonde woman who spoke Spanish fluently but with a strong British accent wanted to discuss her work. Anna and her jealous fit were nowhere to be found. My sister was happy chatting with the blonde woman, so at some point I left them to it and joined my mother and Julian, who were wandering aimlessly with their glasses of wine. Years later, the woman tracked Leandra down to buy a series of photographs. She was a collector who specialised in Latin American women artists and her collection was spread among different museums around the world; she bought one of Leandra's first series. Jacinta was very impressed that my sister had spoken with the woman. It wasn't until after she and Leandra had finished their conversation that Jacinta told my sister that she was *the* collector, that she had an enormous house next to the Victoria and Albert Museum in London, that her dinner parties were world famous and were attended by artists and gallerists who adored her and sought her out.

Jacinta knew someone who'd snuck into one of the woman's opulent parties and had confirmed that she had an impressive collection of art by Latin American women, as well as a collection of first editions from Latin America because her daughter had declared that she wanted to be a writer; the collector had given birth to her on a trip to

Buenos Aires but she was a British citizen. Jacinta knew that the collector's daughter spoke perfect Spanish. She'd heard a few things and had read others in the tabloids she flipped through in line at the supermarket; she hadn't realised the collector was in Mexico, but she recognised her that night from the photos she'd seen of her with all kinds of celebrities.

When Leandra joined us, my mother asked her about her friend Anna. Leandra, who had only referred to her by name before that, said, She's not my friend, Mum, she's my girlfriend, and she left because she got jealous over nothing. Then the four of us went to eat churros with chocolate for dinner at a little place downtown. My mother used to like taking us there with my father when we were in the neighbourhood; her father had taken her and her siblings there when they were kids.

At the table, Leandra told us that she didn't understand why Anna had to be so jealous, why she had to take everything so seriously. You have no idea how she gets, she said, looking at Julian, she just shuts down. Obviously, she went on, I'm the one who does everything wrong and she's a saint who never makes a single mistake. Leandra got a message from Anna and didn't respond. While Julian and my mother talked, she and I speculated about the love life of the photographer who had flirted with her. Her phone rang and she looked at it. That must be Anna calling from some different number, she said, I'll be right back. She went outside for a few minutes and when she came back she whispered to me that it was the guy from the show, that he'd gotten her number from Jacinta. He'd asked her why she'd left without saying goodbye, and if she wanted to get together some time. My sister was happy and her mood was like a magnet drawing the best of that night to her like iron filings.

15

I've had these visions since I was a little girl and my visions look like the films. I've been to the films, there's none in San Felipe but they took me to the city for that. The first time I went with some people from England who took me to the city to see the film I'm in, they came here to the town and spent time with me walking through the milpas and smoking tobacco with me, we ate the food my sister Francisca cooked and they asked me questions like you're asking me, with their interpreters and their machines, they recorded me with the big machines they brought and they recorded Apolonia and Aparicio in the milpas, Aniceta and Francisca wouldn't let the people from England record them, but when they asked Paloma questions she answered them and when the interpreter finished asking questions she asked herself more so they would keep recording her with their machines, they recorded a ceremony I did to cure a young boy of his sickness with herbs and they went with me to the mountain to get herbs to make a Wine for another little boy with a suffering the sages of medicine couldn't cure, they wanted to watch how I cured the boy.

I gave them all cigarettes and sweet coffee like my father Felisberto liked, Apolonia offered them food and the interpreter told me the gentlemen from England thought she was beautiful, Aniceta hid like a mouse in the store because there were machines and people here, my sister Francisca worked the harvest with Aparicio, Paloma made the interpreter laugh, he was a skinny boy the English people brought with them and he looked like a gust of wind could send him flying like an empty plastic bag and with Paloma he never stopped laughing and turning red, because Paloma began right away to talk about her nights and the young interpreter turned red each time. One time they were getting their big machines ready and Paloma said to the interpreter, Love, I've had sex simply because I'm polite. I couldn't get a man to leave my house once and because I'm so polite I said, well, sweetheart, you might as well stay, and then of course I had to offer him the blanket of my warmth. Guadalupe sometimes went to the mountain and left his house to Paloma, he didn't go at night with other Muxes, he didn't need to, there are people who need to and people who don't, I've seen it with many people and Guadalupe didn't need to go at night and it didn't matter to him, Paloma never told him when she went at night with other men and she was happy like that, she liked being with other men and she liked having her home with Guadalupe, right away Paloma told the interpreter about her nights and the boy saw that she was Muxe, you could see that right away, she had him inside her coop and she was tossing him seeds to see if he would peck at one, but the young interpreter only turned red.

Apolonia taught herself to speak a little Spanish and Paloma talked in Spanish with the interpreter, too, and that was how they spoke with the man who brought the people, the man who came to make the film. Aniceta had taught herself too, but she didn't say anything, and Aparicio only said bad words and no one understood him. The interpreter studied languages at a university in England and he spoke my language well, you know they use different words on the other side of the river, and also on the other side of the mountains they use different words, and the interpreter used words we don't use here, but I understand the interpreters they bring me, and this one translated poetry from Mazatec and Zapotec and Mixe into English at his university and he was skinny as a twig and he turned red when he talked, he wore the huaraches he bought in town with white socks and I said to him, why are you wearing socks with your huaraches, you don't eat tacos with a fork and knife, do you? But then the next day he came into my house, he had to bend forward because he was too big for the door and he brought me something from the town so I didn't say anything more about his socks, the boy had good intentions, he didn't know how to wear our things but he did know how to speak our languages like he was from here, it was like that big pale boy was born here in the mountains, of all the people from foreign places he was the one who most understood our languages.

Paloma was in the film and because of her the film theatre filled with Muxes who brought their energy and shouting and celebrations when we went to see the film in the city, you can imagine how Paloma dressed herself up and how she dressed up Apolonia to go. The young interpreter went with me and sat with us, and he told me everything they said before the film and after, when people asked questions and the Englishman answered.

When I watched myself smoking in the milpa, there in the film theatre because that's how the film began, I felt strange. How can I explain it? Paloma put mirrors in my house, she said Feliciana, sweetheart, your girls are so beautiful and you and Francisca are so beautiful, you can't just go outside like a goat's fart without checking your sparkle first, love. And I thought the mirrors Paloma put in our house were beautiful, not because I liked to look at myself in them, I don't care about looking at myself, but everything is reflected in them and I think that's beautiful because it's like mirrors were made by the hand of God, the way God made the stones and the rivers that run, and also the mirrors that return their reflections to us. Seeing yourself in the films is nothing like seeing yourself in a mirror but in a ceremony you reflect up close like in a mirror. In dreams you see yourself do things, you see the things you do and it feels strange to see yourself in dreams because you get close to things but you can't grab them, you can't wake up with something you brought out of the dream because dreams are reflections. In films one image follows another follows another follows another and you can't grab anything like in dreams, but everything we see did happen, you lived and you live what you see, that's what my visions are like, like the films. Dreams are as light as birds and you forget your dreams quickly because they fly away but you don't forget what you see in the films because you lived it, that's how the visions are. We don't take anything with us of the visions we live but they bring us a message that we do take with us, just like we don't take anything with us from this life because nothing on this earth belongs to us, everything we have is loaned to us by God, everything we have carries His name and we leave it all on this earth when we go because all of it is borrowed and if we take anything with us, it's His word, and that word we can see in the ceremony.

Paloma was happy. She said, Feliciana, I'm a film star, love, in the film I talk about my father Gaspar who passed the gift of healing to me in my blood, but I tell you, the sugar I carry in my blood to sweeten this sour world, I made that from my own cane, darling, they should make me my own telenovela like the ones Aniceta watches on the television with that other girl in the store, sweetheart, these English boys should see me at a vela, let me invite them to a vela so they can see me dance, I can light a fire even under the wettest blanket. Aniceta and Francisca said nothing about the film, Aparicio said that his voice didn't sound like a girl's the way it did in the film, but his voice was changing and he was angry. I don't know where children learn so much from their dead because Nicanor was angry that same way when he came back from the war, the way Aparicio was angry with the change in his voice. Paloma said to me, she said, Feliciana, darling, this film made you famous, love, that's why all these handsome men are coming here from all over, these men who come to meet you are so handsome I'm going to buy myself one of those things to take pictures of them and sell them in the market, sweetheart, I'll put my red kiss on them and I'll sell them for more coins that way, love.

Many people came to see me, they spoke other languages and came from other lands to find me. People came from all over, people came from universities in England and the United States and Japan, they came wanting me to teach them about the mushrooms, they wanted me to teach them through their interpreter who was a woman my size they brought from Japan and who had hair as dark and shiny as a cloudless night, she said to me, Feliciana, how can we take care of the mushrooms so we can bring them back to our laboratory in Japan, she said to me serious the way Aparicio was serious as a boy after we put him in his pit in the milpa. The men who came to study the mushrooms said things to her in their language so they could learn how to take care of the mushrooms in their laboratory in Japan, and I said to them and to the interpreter with hair like the cloudless night sky, I said: It's the other way around, the mushrooms take care of you, bring them with you so they can take care of you in Japan for me. And the Japanese men laughed, the interpreter told them these things and they laughed, they didn't understand what I was telling them but their interpreter who was my size and very serious did not laugh, she said everything I said like it was a sermon.

And people came who wanted to take me to Europe to talk there, they told me, Feliciana, come talk to the people in the universities because they want to meet you. Paloma said to me, she said, Feliciana, love, let's go with the güeros, I'll tell Guadalupe that we're going to the Sierra Tarahumara to heal sick elders, but instead we'll go on a little trip with the güeros and take pictures of ourselves all over, darling, so we can look beautiful all around the world. I have no papers, Paloma has no papers, but the people offered us papers so we could travel. I listened to them humble because they wanted me to go talk to the people in the universities in Europe, I listened humble for their good intentions, grateful to them and to God, but I have never left this place because this is my home, this is what I do, what I do isn't talk to people in universities or travel to foreign places. For the travel I do I don't need to leave my little hut, the travel I do is with the Language. Paloma wanted to travel the world, she wanted to go anywhere they would take her and she told a group of people from France to take her and Guadalupe with them, Who's Guadalupe? they asked her and Paloma said, He's my husband but I can go alone. But they didn't want to take Paloma with them, no matter how much she flattered them or made them laugh. I told them, Take Paloma, her blood is the same as mine, she inherited the same things from my grandfather and my great-grandfather, she taught me everything I know, Paloma was the one who told me that the Book was mine, and Paloma looked at the people from France and I said to them, She can teach people in the auditoriums of Europe a lot because here in our town Paloma is the one who teaches us all, but the people from France didn't want to take her, and Paloma gave me a kiss because I gave her a hand with the people from France.

And yes, those musicians from Argentina also came, Paloma told me they were very famous even though she didn't really know why, someone in town told her so and the whisper travelled because people came from the city when they heard that the musicians from Argentina were on their way. Those three young men whistled at all the girls and many young people followed them around and sang their songs. Apolonia didn't know their music, but she got nervous when the young man with the voice said hello to her, I saw her always look down when they were near, the air around them was big, and not unkind but it was strong, I can see the strength in a person's air even if they don't say what they do, even if they don't say a word. We all have our air around us when we're born, some people's you can see just by looking. What I saw in their two ceremonies was that they were simple boys and the air that surrounded them was big, the biggest belonged to the young man with the voice, what I see in these airs is creation, not fame or applause, but creation and the trace it leaves and those are the big airs I'm telling you about, those are the airs I see right away when artists come to me. And in that same way I saw a trace on a poet who came from the city to see me, a güero poet with a great trace and I told him it was creation. If someone is born with creation in the air that surrounds them, it doesn't matter how they dress, it doesn't matter if a sage of medicine is wearing his white coat, what matters is that he has creation in his air, what matters are his actions and his creations because those are what bring strength, the people who see them know that the strength is there, and the three musicians from Argentina had those airs and they got along well together, you could see that they understood each other. Paloma sang with them in my house, they played Mexican songs they knew and Paloma also knew, the picture you asked about, a young man who came with them took that, I didn't make a ceremony for him but he was very nice and he sent Paloma that photograph she kept by her mirror with pictures of other famous people, I didn't want to be in that photograph with the musicians from Argentina but Paloma did. I made two ceremonies for them with mushrooms and later they sent me a record with songs on it that were inspired by those ceremonies, they told me one of the songs was dedicated to me. One of them had just lost his mother, a mother who gave him his first guitar and in the ceremony I saw her teaching him to play the guitar in a bathroom as white as the mist when it comes down off the mountain, that's how white the bathroom was and cold, because his mother said music sounds better in the bathroom. The young man covered his face with his hands when I said that to him. Here is the record you asked me about that the musicians sent me from Argentina but I have no way to listen to its music here, my sister Francisca keeps all the things people send me, music, papers, newspapers, books. I can't read them, but I appreciate books because they're all alike in their form just like all people are alike in form and I appreciate books because they're all like the Book and because all books are children of the Language.

And yes, there was also the man who drew films for children, who showed us his drawings and later brought us things with that little boy and his guitar on them, he sent other things when he was back in the United States after the ceremony we had with the Book. His grandfather also raised him, I had my father Felisberto but my grandfather Cosme raised me, my father died from the pneumonia that took him away and I loved my grandfather Cosme like my father, even though I honour my father every day with my work because if you honour your ancestors then your feet are firm on the earth, and the man who drew films for children, his grandfather also raised him, I saw his house with green all around it, bright green around a white house with many windows, and I saw his mother leave that house, I saw her leave the house and leave her son to his grandfather to raise him, his grandfather gave him coins to go to school and gave him a roof and food, and I saw him talking with his toys and his childhood things and that was where his children's films began, that became his work and with his first creation he bought his grandfather a house, he told me that, it wasn't something I saw, but I saw the house he lived in when he was young and I told him the words he said to his toys, and after the ceremony he made one of the things he said to his toys after his mother left him into a film for children. He sent letters that were read to me the way Nicanor's letters were read to me when he was in the war with the revolutionary soldiers, the artist's letters were always very kind, the man who drew films for children was always very grateful. I don't remember the name of the film for children, but you can find it in your machines, a film for children that the artist saw in his mind during his ceremony. In his walkings the idea came to him from the Day of the Dead. Those things that had always chased him in his dreams, those things that chased him in his bad dreams, he made peace with them, he said, and he went away peaceful because he saw when his mother left him, he saw why his mother left home and the things that he said to his toys helped him understand where he was when he came to see me, because that is what the Language does: it puts things in order, like the spring that follows the winter to unblock the seedlings, the Language also carries the fertile days of summer, The Language puts in order the things you've lived and so you see the present clear. He still sends my grandchildren little things of his creation, the man who drew films for children wanted my children to take their children to see his films in the United States, he wanted to pay for a trip so my children could go to the United States, but my daughters didn't want to and Aparicio asked for the coins instead of the trip. Later the artist who drew films for children had someone bring me to the city so I could watch the film he made from the ceremony, I went with my daughter Aniceta who understood it and told me some parts, Aparicio couldn't bring my grandson and Paloma didn't want to go with us, she said the only thing she liked about children was when they grew up to be men.

The man who drew films for children heard that my grandson Aparicio couldn't go to see his film, so he sent machines from the United States for him to watch it at home, but the machines used more electricity than our cable can lift, the electricity climbs up the gully like a mule climbs heavy with its load, the cable carries its load of electricity slow and heavy upward and like the mule it stumbles backward because the load is so heavy and we spent days without light because we connected one of those machines to it, the smaller one where the film went inside, but that cable couldn't bear even the rains, it was like an old mule with a bad leg, the cable was fragile, the most fragile thing in the house was that electricity cable and so my grandson Aparicio couldn't see the film that the man who drew films for children made after his ceremony with me. After I watched the film for children with Aniceta, I sent a message to the artist with a few words and he sent me a letter back with coins in it, but that wasn't what I wanted, I wanted to tell him what I thought about his film.

A writer also came to see me and later she sent me

her book in English in a yellow envelope with her beautiful purple writing on it, when she came to see me she told me that she always writes in purple, she believes in the hours when people are born, the stars that looked down on the birth, she said that the stars that see our birth are the ones that light our future, and I couldn't say anything about that, but she believed so deeply in hours and stars and purple was her colour because she said it was the colour of the stars that saw her birth and just like she wrote in purple she dressed all in red because she said that the colour red protected her and she used purple to write because it was like words were being born from the colour of her birth and I look at her book and I think it's beautiful because of all the colours on the cover, it has her colours, red and purple on the cover, and I know the book is beautiful and I imagine my ancestors would also like to look at it, even though like me they don't know how to read and we never learned Spanish or English because why should we learn other tongues, here no one wants to learn the government's tongue and we don't want to wear their city clothes, and just like we stay far from their tongue and their clothes, we want them to stay far from ours because we have our tongue and clothes just like we have our blood and ancestors. The writer's book is beautiful and so is the yellow envelope because she drew purple mushrooms on it and because of that I saved it inside the book. She sensed that the mushrooms were connected one to another and I liked that because I see them the same way, this is why I join them in unions when I find them there on the hillside, and this is what she drew in purple on her yellow envelope. Later she sent me the book in Spanish but I couldn't read that either, and my children don't read Spanish even though they can speak some. I look at the Spanish book, I look at the cover and I tell you, it's ugly. Just like how there are people in families, of a girl's eight children, only one of them might harvest the beauty of their grandparents and great-grandparents, the way a rich man shows off his gold, that's how the one who harvests the beauty of their ancestors shows off their appearance, just like that, there's one who harvests the ugliness, you can look and look and not find any charm, that's the child who harvests the worst in the appearances of all the relatives who were born before, and that's how ugly the book was that the writer sent me in Spanish, and how beautiful the one was that she sent me in her tongue.

My sister Francisca was toasting chillies on the comal, we had beans, atole, squash, and tamales, Paloma and Guadalupe ate with us and I showed her the book and said it was ugly and she said, Feliciana, love, look at this jumble of words, I hope they don't have the things in their houses all heaped up in a jumble like the words in this book, because they would all be spilling out the windows, these books are good for one thing and that's for putting under pots on the table so the pots don't burn the wood. Paloma didn't care if books were beautiful or ugly, all she cared about was beautiful men but she tried to follow along, she was always with me no matter what we were doing because Paloma was loyal. I tell you no one was as loyal as her. I didn't say anything to the writer, her job is what goes inside the books, just like how salted beans make the taco, and the writer is a beautiful person and she has the air of creation, one day she brought her son so I could meet him when they were visiting a beach nearby, her son and her husband came and she said, I want you to meet my son, and I gave them sweet coffee and I smoked a cigarette with her husband here in my house, and I gave them herb mixtures, they asked me to make them a Wine and they thanked me many times because the boy had gotten a sickness in his stomach when he ate a bad piece of fish on the beach, and that was when she told me that her book had taken her on journeys to different countries thanks to the journey she took here in my hut, thanks to the creations that came from her ceremony. She is a beautiful person, I saw that inside her and in the air that surrounded her.

My sister Francisca saves all the articles in a crate over there, all the books in different tongues, the university papers, and I look at them, I touch them and I flip through their pages, I like their colours, they seem good to me and

I like the smell of the books more than the magazines because the magazines smell like selling, I smoke my cigarette and see myself in the black and white photographs you spoke of, the photographs taken by a gringo who spent time with me asking me about when I was a child, he asked me about my father Felisberto when he took the photograph where I'm smoking in black and white, the ember from my cigarette looks white in those photographs so it brings me the image of sugar when it falls on the ground more than the image of fire, but they say the stars are gathered fire and at night from far away they look like that, like sugar spilled on the ground on a starry night, and I see myself in those pictures from the gringo photographer with the end of my cigarette glowing white, many photographers portrait me like that because I tell them better to do it like that than in my ceremonies, I say you can't photograph the Language, why they want to take my picture I don't know, it would be good to take a picture of the Language because that is what the ceremony is made of, but take your picture of me with my cigarette because that you can record just like photographs can record the white stars in the distance like sugar spilled on the ground.

One-eyed Tadeo wanted to take advantage when he heard the gringo banker had come here with his wife, I don't know how One-eyed Tadeo heard about the things they brought and the people who came, back then the musicians and the artists hadn't come yet, none of the people who came after the gringo banker and his wife the sage of medicine came, none of those people had come yet, they were the ones who brought all the people who came after the people from England made their film, but when the banker and his wife came to see me One-eyed Tadeo heard the clinking of coins, he heard the coins that the banker Tarsone and his wife had and right away he went to find them to take them to his hut to tell them the future with his kernels of corn and his cards that he used so he could say he saw the future with his bad eye.

The gringo banker and his wife saw that film in New York, where they were from, and they got an interest in me and in my path of healing with the Language, with herbs and mushrooms. He was already interested in mushrooms because his wife was a sage of medicine for children and she was very known in the United States because she worked with alternative medicines and she had studied different mushrooms, but she didn't know the mushrooms in Mexico and that was how when their children grew and went to university they started travelling all around the world to search for mushrooms, they gave their money for healings that were not from laboratories and travelled all around the world searching for mushrooms and plants. They worked with penicillin mushrooms, with healing mushrooms from all over because mushrooms from different places have different healing properties, but when the gentlemen from England came to make their film about me they showed it to the banker and his wife and they saw me large there on the screen and they saw the large earth-covered mushrooms from the hillside that I put in my cottoncloth sacks, and even though I couldn't use those mushrooms in any ceremony because the people with recording machines had seen them, I could explain how I used them while I cleaned the earth from them and put them away safe, and I also took them to the hillside between San Juan de los Lagos and San Felipe where I went to walk with my father Felisberto before he died, where the mushroom Children grow and in the rains so many grow there that no sack can hold them, and the banker and his wife saw them large on the screen and they found the men from England, and the man who made the film told them that they had come to my house every day for a time on the backs of mares and mules, that they had paid people from town to come to the gully with their machines and their things so they could put everything in the film because they wanted to put my whole life in, I remember I laughed when the young interpreter told me that, well, that night in the celebrations after the film the gentleman from England told the banker and his wife more about me and told them how to get to where we live here in San Felipe.

And that was how I met Mr Tarsone, whom people

started calling Mister Tarzan as soon as he set foot in San Felipe. I tell you, right away One-eyed Tadeo heard the clinking of the coins they brought and he went around saying Mister Tarzan this and Mister Tarzan that and he met the banker and his wife before I met them and he told them lies, but someone in town told them that One-eyed Tadeo was a liar and not to give him any coins and that person brought them here to me because they had journeyed all this way to meet me. Mr Tarsone treated me with respect and gratitude from the moment he told me his name. I made a ceremony for both of them, for him and for his wife who studied alternative healings for children, just looking at them I could see there was something they needed to find. In that ceremony their two children appeared and she saw everything they had of her in them, just as clear as water when it separates from oil, she saw everything she liked about herself and everything she didn't like about herself that was in her children, and he saw his mother. They came to me many times, they took notes and photographs and asked me if they could record my songs I sang with the Language in a ceremony, and I told them yes. Mr Tarsone brought a machine and he brought people to record me with it. They came again and again to my house from where they lived here in San Felipe and on one of those comings Mrs Tarsone said to me, Feliciana, we're going to build you a house, and they started having a house built for us. When she said it to me I said no, we have a house already, I didn't want to accept it, even though I accepted all the other things people gave me, humbly, the Tarsones and the others. The small and big coins from all around the world, the liquor, the tobacco, the food they brought us and the things for my three children, for my sister Francisca, for Paloma and Guadalupe, even for my mother, may she rest in peace, who got things when I first began because it brought kindnesses to us all. That was how they paid for my ceremonies, the people who came to see me paid me with kindnesses, but I never put a price on what I do, I can't put a price on it because what I do has no price, it would be the same as to put a price on walking, it isn't possible, but also I have a family and they all shelter with me, so I was grateful for the house they wanted to make for us. When the Tarsones sent the materials and the men to build the house, I knew that it was a gift from them and also a gift from God, and I thanked them and I thanked God because gifts are blessings. Mr Tarsone was grateful to me and said that the house was nothing, that the ceremonies had given more to them. He said, Feliciana, you and your family have given us much more, and he sent me an interpreter with a beard and a moustache to ask me where I wanted things in the house they were building, and every time the interpreter with the beard and the moustache came to see me I offered him tobacco and sweet coffee, the way my father Felisberto drank it. Guadalupe brought a bottle of liquor to break on the wall for the celebrations, Paloma brought her friends from the velas, Aniceta brought the woman who owned the store and her relatives, people came to eat the tamales my sister Francisca made. I was happy when we came here to live. My daughter Apolonia married a young man and they lived here with their two daughters, all of us fit in the house I made how I wanted it with the help of the interpreter with a beard and a moustache, one time I healed a sickness in the interpreter's back with a prayer and with holding my hand to his back I healed him, he had appreciation and respect for me because he said the sages of medicine couldn't cure the suffering in his back and he was very grateful, he came with men in helmets who put all the corners where they should corner and all the windows where I wanted them, in their gratitude the Tarsones sent beds, we never had beds before, they also sent us many things we never knew how to use and many things we never wanted to learn how to use, and my son Aparicio right away got a taste for the things they sent, even though he and his girl didn't know how to use them, either, they got a taste for these things and took many of them to their own house, and Paloma took some things too because she wanted to sell them at the market, she and Guadalupe sold them and bought clothes for the night and clothes for the day and alcohol for the cold.

No, I told them, no you can't take the dirt floor and the thatch from the hut where I made my ceremonies, the interpreter with a beard and a moustache wanted to do that but the hut is just the same as when I started my ceremonies, as when I healed the first people they brought me, and healed my sister Francisca when death laid its egg in her, and that was where I made a ceremony for Guadalupe when I saw he carried his father buried inside him because his father humiliated him when he was wearing a tunic as bright orange as a fire at night, my hut carries all my healings inside it, all the words the Language has healed, and so my hut is like the Book, inside are all the times I used the Language to heal and inside the hut is where all those times live.

The Tarsones sent us clothes from the United States. I told them I like to smoke, I like my coffee sweet like my father Felisberto drank it because that way I talk to him every day and give him thanks, I like to drink liquor with Paloma but then I have to cleanse myself, and this is how I have always been, I'm not going to change my clothes or my huaraches, no one is going to put clothes from the United States on me, I am not awed by things and I am not awed by power, the way I see some people awed by the power of coins, I like what I do and I use what I need and I need only what God loans to us in this life, nothing more. Some people are awed by things, they are awed by the owning of things and believe that the bigger the pile of things a person owns, the greater the power they have. My daughters and my grandchildren divide the things that people send me from far away, I need only my clothes and my huaraches, my cigarettes, my sweet coffee, the food my sister Francisca makes, I need nothing more than that, than the life that God gave me. I see often that people give me things and go away happy with the idea that they exchanged their experience for the things they give me, people leave here happy because they gave me coins, like the men from the universities who studied the Language and who came and went away happy with the idea that they had learned the Language but I tell you, the Language is new every day, you can't learn it that way because it never stays the same, it's like a cloud that changes with the wind, the wind that multiplies, I told them I work with the Language and I never know what will come next, because the Language is the present and it is as vast as the night, as vast as the present, and this is why the Language that the wind multiplies is powerful, because it is always changing like the clouds are always changing in the sky, the words change their shape, and the men from the university recorded me and took their notes and told me things by their interpreters but not even the interpreters understood what they were saying, and with all the things and all the coins coming in One-eyed Tadeo came and put a bullet in me the day he heard the

Tarsones were going to build me a house, that was the first time that language left me, it has left me two times and the first was then, when Paloma told me that One-eyed Tadeo had put a bullet in me, when I woke up in a white room full of white light and empty of language.

16

Leandra stayed over at Anna's place the night of the opening, after Anna had gotten jealous and made a scene. Mr Big Shot had sent her a message in the morning, which Anna read while Leandra was in the shower. She had another fit. Mr. Big Shot's real name was José, but that was what Anna called him. My sister hadn't responded, which seemed to pique his interest even more. He invented all kinds of reasons to send her messages, until Leandra finally answered him one Friday night while she was work-ing in her dark room. They went out for a beer that same night. If Anna called the house, I was instructed to tell her that Leandra was asleep.

Sometime around then, Anna took Leandra to meet her mother; the next time they went, they invited me and Julian to join them. Anna's mother lived alone in a small red brick house with wooden frames around the windows and a floating wooden staircase, identical to the maybe twenty other houses in her gated community, which was across from a cemetery and near a ravine. It was far from down-town and even without traffic it took us a good hour and a half to get there by taxi. At the bottom of the ravine there was a river that smelled like stagnant water; the house smelled of mildew and the eucalyptus you could see through the round bathroom window. Anna's mother seemed like a kind person, but that day she'd made a gratuitous biting comment about Anna's father and I didn't understand where it had come from. We sat around the table talking for a long time after the midday meal, then went upstairs with Anna to watch a film and look at photographs in rustic wooden frames. All the pictures were of Anna and her mother. When we got home, Leandra told me that Anna's mother had fought with everyone in her family, more or less like how our father had stopped talking to his brother, but Anna's mother never spoke to her family again and on top of that, she had a combative relationship with her ex-husband. That night, as we were getting changed for bed, Leandra shared a few things with me that she'd noticed about Anna's relationship with her mother, who seemed extremely possessive of her only child. She told me a few anecdotes about the two of them, but neglected to mention that she'd seen José that morning.

I realised that she and José were still in touch one day when I heard her talking on the phone in the bathroom with the door closed, which was pretty unusual for her. My theory was that Leandra saw José in part because Anna had planted the seed in their arguments, that her dramas pushed her jealous fantasies into the realm of reality, and also in part because I think my sister was more attracted to him than she wanted to admit.

My mother spent a lot of time with my aunt and often visited her after work. She'd take Rumba for a walk when she got home if neither of us was around. She gave us plenty of freedom, as long as she always knew where we were. I think my father would have given us a similar kind of freedom, even though he was more strict, but he also would have wanted us to spend more time with him. My father was more demanding, he had a way of putting things that usually got me or Leandra to change our Friday plans and go to Home Depot with him. Maybe because her household had been so oppressive when she was growing up, my mother cut us a lot of slack and preferred to invite my aunt to her work functions, rather than making us go with her. Leandra spent more time at Anna's, and Julian and I were more often at home.

Anna lived in a flat with two friends from the university she met thanks to some flyers she'd put up near the entrances to the main library. One of them was older, she was twenty-nine and pursuing her doctorate in aesthetics. Her room was the biggest and had a balcony facing a rubber tree, so she paid more than the other two. Anna's other flatmate, Simona, was twenty-five and had bright orange hair and a piercing in her lower lip; she had tattoos and tattooed other people, she was the one who bleached and dyed Anna's blue pompadour, and she made more as a tattoo artist in her spare time than she did at her office job in the architecture department at the university. Leandra, Julian and I were a few years younger than they were, and we envied their apartment. One afternoon Simona called Julian to ask if we wanted to stop by for a few beers when we got off work at the newspaper. Simona had just finished rolling a joint when Anna appeared, bawling, to say that she and Leandra had just broken up. She didn't even notice that Julian and I were sitting there.

As soon as she could, Leandra took the entry exam for the art school Julian attended, applied for a Young Artist scholarship, and – without breaking her promise to my father – got a tattoo. My sister had dumped Anna because of Anna's jealousy issues, but their relationship didn't end because of José. She'd seen him a few times, they hung out and sent each other messages, but nothing had happened between them. It's not as if moral scruples stopped my sister from taking things further, it just didn't happen. The scholarship she received before starting at the university not only provided her with a grant, it also meant she'd spend three weekends over the course of the year discussing her project with other grant recipients for three weekends over the course of the year, and talking about their projects with small groups of grantees who worked in the same discipline. On the first night of the first one of these week-ends, Leandra sent me a text message from her hotel room.

— someone told my roommate i set a school on fire and now shes scared of me

— Tell her it's a lie, you burnt down a hotel full of young artists.

— haha this place is great you know in the bus this morning they sat us by last name and i was next to a super cool poet, we spent the whole day talking about our work and there's a party in one of the painters rooms now I have to shower and pick up some beers with my poet friend

— I didn't get the chance to tell you, but Anna reached out to Julian this afternoon, she wants to go for a coffee with him.

— pffffft i didn't get the chance to tell you either but she tracked mum down at work

As part of her scholarship, Leandra made a series of photographs of professions on the verge of disappearing. She continued the project at the university, and later it would be the project she submitted to complete her degree. She brought photos of a few of the workers to that first weekend, but Leandra's project really focused on their workspaces, tools, utensils, desks, and the products of their labour. Still, what she brought with her were photos of a woman who made paper flowers, a man who owned a letterpress and made business cards, and an older woman who'd run a travel agency since the 1950s. I stayed up late reading, and in the middle of the night I started getting more text messages from Leandra.

— SIS U THERE???

— What's up?

— what do u think of José???

— Mr Big Shot?

— yeah

— I don't know him, I only saw him once.

— am gonna introduce youuuuu

Leandra sent me pictures of a room full of people – some of them were dancing, some smoking – and one of a shower cap stretched over a smoke detector to keep it from going off. The fact that Leandra would ask me about Mr Big Shot in the middle of all that, and that she didn't call him Mr Big Shot, tipped me off to what was coming. José was thirty-one and recently divorced; his marriage had lasted two years after a long engagement. By then my sister had stopped working at the dentist's office, she was still in her photography class, but it wouldn't be long before she traded that in for her classes at the university. José was the one who pursued her. They talked on the phone and exchanged text messages, on more than one occasion when I turned out the lights in our room, Leandra's face would stay lit by the screen of her cell phone.

— You're into him, sis.

— nah . . . he's fun, just a friend

— What do you two talk about?

— he's telling me there was a meeting in his office and someone brought all this fancy food iberian ham and french cheeses and his dog jumped up and like inhaled a whole plate of ham

— And?

— and then puked the whole thing up on a couch in this goo that smelled like acorns i dunno he's cute sis what do u want me to say

A few days before Leandra left for the Young Artists weekend, Anna sent me an email asking to see me. I agreed to see her but didn't tell my sister, and listened to her but didn't tell her anything about José when she asked. Meanwhile, sparks were beginning to fly between Leandra and José. Anna showed up at the house one Sunday when Leandra wasn't home and wasn't picking up her phone. She dug in her heels, she wanted to talk with Leandra. My mother offered her some leftover noodles and sausage and made her feel comfortable. Anna looked sad and we didn't seem to be much help, just the opposite: being in our presence seemed to underscore the fact that they weren't together anymore. My mother and I agreed not to tell Leandra that Anna had come by, but – true to form – my mother let it slip.

Not long after that Young Artists weekend, Leandra

and José started dating. One day she asked me to pick her up on my way home without telling me I'd be meeting her at José's place. José answered the intercom and invited me up for a beer. He'd rented a small apartment, there were a few bookshelves and small piles of books on the floor. All the light was indirect except for a bare bulb in the kitchen hanging from two colourful cables stuck together with electrical tape, which made me think of Julian's theory of lightbulbs.

I picked my sister up at that apartment several times. José didn't have much furniture, but there were lots of big plants that seemed like something out of a jungle and a big, honey-coloured dog that seemed remarkably well-behaved compared to Rumba – my mother had started calling her The Stapler for all the tooth marks she'd left in our furniture. José worked for a film production company and wanted to be an artist. The first time I went to pick her up there, I noticed that she was more into him than she could admit; she was attracted to him sexually, I could tell from the way they interacted, but as soon as we got into the car it was harder to tell where she stood.

— can u believe they only fucked in two positions all those years they were together?

— He told you that???

— course not but there are things u just know

— Well, you know, there's no accounting for taste.

— theres something that makes me uncomfortable tho when I'm with him. it wasn't like that with Anna, you know?

— Do you miss Anna?

— are u nuts? josé's awesome

Leandra got back together with Anna a little while after that. My sister sent her a drunken text message from a party she'd gone to with José. Anna wrote her back in the morning and they shut themselves in her room in the apartment; they talked for a whole weekend, Anna forgave her, and Leandra hung José out to dry.

Leandra and Anna were together for around five years after that separation. Anna opened a veterinary clinic with a few classmates from her course in a great location and started spending more time at the house; my sister started showing up with new tattoos, one of which Simona had done before moving out of the flat she shared with the post-grad. Anna started showing up with new scars from her patients at the clinic. Rumba started spending more time there, too. Right near the door there was a big, soft dog bed covered in tartan fabric. Anna had saved a stray dog on a busy avenue, it had managed to dodge several cars but in the end it had gotten hit and Anna had needed to stitch up a pretty big wound. Leandra named it El Chapo that same day. Rumba and El Chapo got along great, they hung out together at the clinic. My mother loved Anna and Julian equally and included them in our family plans; even though she had her own life and her outings with my aunt, she enjoyed it when we ate dinner at the house or invited her to something we were doing. I spent one Christmas in Chihuahua with Julian, and he spent two with us, one at my aunt's place, and the other at my father's brother's home, where we met our cousins' boyfriends. One of them had recently become engaged to a notary and my aunt made a point of saying several times that both of his parents were successful notaries, each with their own practice. That was the Christmas when Leandra invited Anna and her mother to one of our family gatherings. My mother got along well with Anna's, though my uncle and aunt were cold from the start and my cousin insisted on explaining our relationship with Anna and her mother to her fiancé in a weird, defensive way. Leandra made a few funny remarks and had the notary eating out of the palm of her hand.

I broke up with Julian when he moved to Chihuahua, just before I finished my degree and just after I got my own apartment. A little while after things ended with Julian, maybe three or four months, I got drunk at a party and made out with a guy I'd just met; I didn't remember giving him my number, or wanting to, but he wrote to me the next day and that was the week Rogelio and I started dating. From the start, it was clear that he was trouble. He'd lie to me and go out with his friends, and every now and then he'd convince me I was making things up that he himself had said, but even with his problematic behaviour and the pit I was in, we managed to spend a few nice weekends together watching films, talking until late, going out. In retrospect, I see that brief relationship as a necessary low point that had nothing to do with Rogelio, really, it was about my mourning, which hit me with a delay. Actually, it was only recently with Feliciana that I was able to see the missing piece of the puzzle. Leandra had always played that role in our family, my father suffered every time they kicked her out of a school, my mother suffered every time she was insolent or rebelled against authority – I think deep down my mother trusted more in who Leandra was, but my father was deeply worried she would get caught out in the game of musical chairs because of her behaviour, which had nothing to do with her undeniable talents. My sister was a ticking time bomb and it only takes one of those to blow up a house. Maybe that's why my explosion was slow and internal.

Before they kicked Leandra out of her third school, it seemed like she might have been on the road to redemption. The director spoke with my parents and said that despite having the fire on her record, one of Leandra's teachers had negotiated for her to be able to stay at the school, on the condition that she undergo psychological evaluation for her behaviour. They gave her a few tests and sent her to therapy. It turned out that she was way above average intelligence. We'd already known that, but it was striking to see the graphs. She had the intelligence of someone ten years older than her, but the emotional responses of a little girl. In particular, the psychological evaluation indicated that there was no reason to expect Leandra to set anything else on fire or cause any further destruction of property, and that there was no reason to think she was a danger to herself or anyone else, which we also already knew. That was her pass to go back to school, even though they still kicked her out later for misbehaving. My father begged Leandra, blinking furiously to hold back his tears, to finish school once and for fucking all. And she did.

I miss my father when I see Leandra's work circulate. I know that no one would have been happier than him at where she is at thirty-two, how far she's come doing something that he would have liked to have done, and I think it would have made him even happier that it's his little Lea doing it than if he'd have done it himself. I suspect that her relationship with Anna would have been tougher for him at first, but he would have supported her and I think he would've liked Leandra's current girlfriend, Tania. He might not be quite as enthusiastic, though, about how Leandra still wears that fire like a medal, how the fire she started with the Zippo Spectrum she'd been given to light her First Communion candle is one of the few things she's truly proud of.

17

I woke up in a white hospital room, that was the only time a sage of medicine healed me, he took out the bullet One-eyed Tadeo had put in my shoulder. My daughter Apolonia had already gone to complain to him that the boy she liked went to the store with his pregnant wife and the swine tried something, drunk as he was, and my daughter Apolonia sent him to the ground with one kick. It became a problem because my son Aparicio is full of spite, the spite rises fast in him and he went to One-eyed Tadeo's house and he kicked him, but not like my daughter had kicked him, Aparicio went to his house to kick him in his face hard for the bullet Tadeo put in my shoulder and also for the lies he told Apolonia, even though time had passed Aparicio doesn't forget those things, his spite grows in him like bushes grow in the rains and with that same anger he carried since One-eyed Tadeo heard they were building us a house and put a bullet in me, Aparicio gave him a hard kicking but he didn't end him there on the ground, drunk as he was, Aparicio chose not to end One-eyed Tadeo, who couldn't defend himself because of all the liquor that swelled him, because I had told my son, the death of a person is only for God to make, and just like he never forgot his spite I told him that this was something he should never forget.

They took me to a hospital in town to see a sage of medicine and that's where I woke up and saw Paloma, and the sage of medicine said to me, Feliciana, my name is Salvador, we'll talk with the help of an interpreter. I was awed by his conduct, I was awed by everything I saw in his name when he told it to me, I saw that he was a man who had saved many lives and that he recently saved a child who was born from a split in his mother's belly, he brought into the world that child born without breath, I saw the baby's cries caught in his throat and his grey skin fresh pulled from the split in the belly of his mother who was fading, the child with his mouth open but no breath passing through, he wanted to breathe but he couldn't, his mouth was open but no air would go in, I saw that Salvador had saved that baby but I couldn't tell him that because people get scared, the way it happened when I was a little girl and Fidencio who sold thatch started to cry when I touched his arm and told him that I saw a white dog running towards a hill and he got angry with me, and so now I don't tell people when I see things. Instead I told him, You are a great doctor, Salvador, because the Language made you one with your name. Salvador took the bullet out of me and he took the pain out of me without any discomfort, I felt no discomfort in my body, and then the next day he said to me, Feliciana, he said, I know who you are, your name is in all the newspapers, your name is known around the world, there's someone who wants to bring you to your home when you leave here, when you are well, someone who wants to meet you and bring you to your home.

The food they gave me during the three nights and three days I was in the hospital was very bad and so I said to Salvador, I said, This food is not God's will, you sages of medicine there in your white coats and the rest of us here eating this food that is not God's will, and he gave me his laughter. I missed my sweet coffee, my tobacco, the squash I planted at home, my chayotes, my beans and the tortillas my sister Francisca makes, the atole she makes me, now that tastes good, that's what I always ate. I told Salvador that this food had burned my comal and in that moment I realised the food we eat at home is home itself. I didn't eat the food from the hospital where the sage of medicine Salvador worked, I chose not to eat that food and to leave there with my skin stuck to my bones and when I got hungry on the third sun I stood up from the white cot, with difficulty but no discomfort, before Paloma came to bring me the tamales she had promised me from the market, I took off the blue rag they had put on me and put on my clothes and I went home.

One afternoon when I was back in my house, a man came to tell me that the doctor from the hospital who had taken the lead out of my shoulder wanted to visit me with a friend of his, and it was strange because the man who came to tell me the message was a man from the government, and he knew who I was. I understood what they wanted and I made preparations for a ceremony, with the help of God I went to the hillside to cut mushrooms for them and for myself and late in the afternoon the doctor arrived with his friend, and the man from the government arrived who had brought me the message, and the interpreter who had helped us communicate in the hospital told me that the doctor Salvador wasn't going to be a part of the ceremony, he wanted only for me to make a ceremony for his friend. I paid no attention, I told him we would eat the mushrooms together and Salvador told me roughly that he didn't want to eat them, and I said to him, you cured me, now I am offering to cure you, Salvador. His friend took my side, the interpreter told me, he said, She wants him to be a part of the ceremony also, but he doesn't want to. His friend encouraged him until the interpreter finally told me that they would both be part of the ceremony and I could see that Salvador was doing it by force. The man from the government waited outside the door for them to come back out.

The doctor Salvador had a face of ash in the ceremony and he cleansed himself of the ash that was the guilt he carried as a doctor and when the ceremony was over he had lost the guilt he carried and that day we became friends. I tell you, Zoe, the ceremony would clean away the guilt you carry, if you choose to have one, the ceremony would let you see what you owe to your father and also what you owe to yourself. The friendship with Salvador took root and later he moved to a big hospital in the city and he would visit me to ask about the sufferings he could not see with his machines, he visited me many times with studies and papers, many times he visited me in the milpa and when I was there with the harvest and my tobacco I would hear him say, Madam Doctor, and I would know who it was and I would say, Salvador, and I would see the face of the man who took from my body the lead of rage that One-eyed Tadeo put in my shoulder because they were building us a house. Salvador would say to me, Feliciana, the house is getting big, they are building it quickly, and I saw that it was bigger and I spent more and more time in the hut where I make my ceremonies with the Language. After he shot me and after my son Aparicio gave him a beating, I greeted One-eyed Tadeo the way I always did. Paloma would say to me, Feliciana, you're a respectable woman, love, don't say hello to that stupid Maraca. But if his wish was to cast a shadow over my house and make it dark then I needed to greet him like the sun every day, even if wars still continued on earth.

The governor went at night with Salvador's friend, I saw that during their ceremony when I understood what that man from the government with his car and his steel for sending bullets was doing at my house, and one day she brought him here to see me. He said to me, Feliciana, I want you to help me with a situation, you are a powerful woman and I need you to help me with my situation. He had gone to a brujo in Veracruz who bathed him in the warm blood of many roosters but could not help him, someone was trying to kill him and he came to me to say, Feliciana, I need you to help me see who wants my hide, help me with your powers. I looked at him, I offered him tobacco, and he told me I should help him with his situation in the government, I should do him favours with my sight, because he knew I could see all. But I told him that all I saw was him standing in front of me and he got angry and left with his man and his steel for sending bullets.

Then his wife came to see me and she said to me, Feliciana, in a dream I saw them burn my husband alive, for the love of God help him, it's heating up around here, come to our house, my husband wants to make you an offering. I told her, I don't go to people's houses because people come to see me. The wife said, Feliciana, he's a good man and those animals want to tear him limb from limb, ask your mushrooms and your herbs who wants to kill him, who is following him, and if you agree to be my husband's bruja he'll give you something big, she said, he'll give you enough coins for you and your children and your grand-children, come with me to see him and he'll make his offering, a grand offering for you and your family, but I said no, I don't need anything more than the person you see in front of you, I don't need his offering. And she looked at me and then she left.

I saw that something was going to happen, I saw that the governor's wife was going to do something. Not her, but her people. I had recovered from the bullet and could move my arm, I was healthy again but did not take the medicines that Salvador gave me, the medicines he brought for me on the day he and his friend came for their cere-mony, I healed myself with herbs I blessed before I picked them from the hillside, the herbs speak to me according to the suffering, I speak the tongue of the herbs and I healed myself that way, and on the morning I woke up healthy after the bullet I saw that grey birds had come to fight in the milpa, they fought with the hens over their corn, they fought hard for the corn and feathers flew through the air from the striking of their beaks and I knew that rage would come to my house because the air, the hills and the clouds, the flowers and herbs, they all carry messages for us, nature carries the Language, you just have to listen, and this rage was the message brought to me by the grey birds that came to fight in the milpa.

That night brought another evil of rage. I don't speak evils with the Language, its powers are great and its good and evil forces are equal in strength, but you can choose the good or the evil and this is why I greeted One-eyed Tadeo the same way before and after the bullet, because I don't speak evils or carry spite, I am grateful to God for the life I have and for lending me the Language to heal people. The house was not yet finished and we were asleep inside in the early hours when I felt a discomfort in the shoulder where the lead had gone in, the discomfort woke me and I knew it was the rage of the governor's wife stabbing into me, and that was when I heard the tongues of fire. The governor's wife had sent people who burned our roof but not our house, so we were able to put out the flames with water. Fire turns water to vapour and water puts out the fire, the fire hushes the water and the water hushes the fire, just like the forces of good and evil can hush one another, and we put the fire out with water to put an end to the evils of rage.

In town they said to Paloma that I was revealing the secrets of our ancestral medicine, that foreigners were coming and that the mushrooms on the hillside now spoke the tongue of the government and other foreign tongues and that it was my fault. Paloma said to me, she said, Feliciana, love, people are saying all kinds of things about you because of the bullet and the fire, One-eyed Tadeo can't stand the house they're building for you or the people who come to see you from all over, the governor and his wife want you to be their bruja so you can do their dirty work, we have to put a stop to this, love.

Paloma sent a message to the Tarsones by the interpreter with a beard and a moustache and a white helmet, he wanted to put iron where the roof was burned and make another one and I said to him that we would have thatch, and I said to my daughter Aniceta to bring the man who sold thatch who was the nephew of Fidencio, the man I made cry when I was a little girl because I told him I saw a white dog running toward the hillside and I believe that what I saw was his dead son. Paloma was worried because the evils continued, she had a dream where she saw more evils coming and she came to me and said, Feliciana, she said, I dreamed that thunder struck the milpa six times. And I said to her, Paloma, animals fight the beast they see as weak, I said, the evils won't return to this house because we are strong and animals don't fight strong beasts. The fire showed me that the evils were a test from God to give me strength, they were not misfortunes to wash me away the way the rains wash the earth from the hillside. One-eyed Tadeo put a bullet in my shoulder, men set tongues of fire to my roof and I saw that when fire licks the hillside it gives its light to the dark, I also saw that the fire that burns the sown field never burns for long and I said, if I don't take my strength from God, next will be my children.

And so I got to my feet, for my sister Francisca I got to my feet and for Paloma, the fire that wounded me also spoke to me, it said, Feliciana, now you are fire and fire can't touch you now because you are the fire. This was what the fire told me that night.

The interpreter with a beard and a moustache and a helmet sent a message to the Tarsones and they sent a message to the governor asking him favours for me and because the sound of coins lights the governor's eyes he came to my house to tell me he was going to investigate who wanted to hurt me. It's your wife, I thought, you're the ones who want to hurt me, but I didn't say those things to the governor. I thanked the Tarsones but I asked them not to go to the governor for favours for me, I was strong enough alone. In her store, someone said to my daughter Aniceta that witches deserve all the fires that come to them, and I said to her, Aniceta, I said, I'm no bruja, I'm no fortune teller and I'm not the future but I am the Language and its words are the present, the Book was given to me, I am the Book Woman and I am the Language, my child.

Yes, the Tarsones came to see me again and again. Then they brought their daughter to meet me. I spoke with her, I saw that she was a student at a nice university, I saw that she had many things with the crest of the university on them, I saw the crests on her clothes, the crest on her coffee cup, I saw that she even had the crest of her nice university on her cigarette lighter and I told the girl when I met her that she should get rid of all those crests from the university, I told her, Throw away those clothes, my child, throw away that coffee cup and that cigarette lighter you have, your nice university doesn't matter, good fortune is yours because you are intelligent, not because of your nice university, and the girl was frightened because the cigarette lighter with the crest of her university was in her pocket and I pointed to it, she wanted to give it to me but I said, No, my child, throw it away.

The daughter did not make a ceremony, she went back to town where the family was staying, and I made a ceremony for the Tarsones. I saw that Mr Tarsone had been very sick as a boy, he had spent more than forty days and forty nights in a hospital where he was connected to machines and I saw him negotiate with a sage of medicine so they wouldn't hurt his arm any more with their needles, I saw him offer his toy to the sage of medicine so they wouldn't stick him in the arm any more and the sage of medicine accepted the toy and stuck him in the other arm and only later they stuck the arm where it hurt again and the sage of medicine gave the toy to the father of young Tarsone, who even as a boy was already a businessman, he negotiated like a lynx, he didn't know all the words yet but he negotiated like a lynx and I saw that he was born for business, he carried business inside him and business carried coins to him.

People ask me, How do you see the past, Feliciana when you say you see the present. And I say that the Language is always the present, even if you speak it in the past, it's still the present. Sometimes the present carries the past and sometimes it carries the future, but it is always the present. For God it is always the present, for us it is always the present, the Language is always the present, and these things I tell you now are what the Tarsones wrote in the newspapers that grew the whispers and brought the foreigners here to San Felipe. They brought people who came to know their deep waters through the Language.

Many people came and I asked each one why but just by looking at them I could see who wanted to know their present and who was searching for their deep waters, I went out there with my cigarette and I smoked and I looked at them and I asked them their name, and just by looking I could see who wanted to be guided by the Language and who was there for entertainment. Paloma said to me, Feliciana, darling, if you're going to do all the serious work, someone has to have fun for you, love, so I'm going to spend my nights in town. Paloma went out almost every night then and almost never came to visit, but the almost never that she came to visit was a help to me.

The musician you said came to see me, he was dressed in dazzling white, the air that surrounded him and his strength were great and he came with his people, Paloma taught him the word for prince in Spanish and he said, Me llamo Príncipe in the government's tongue and Paloma taught his people other words in Spanish. People came, people came with other tongues and they stayed with people from town in their houses, they came with their backpacks and their coins, they gave gifts to the people of San Felipe in exchange for room and board. The governor made streets, he wanted the people from far away to like him, he didn't care if the people from town liked him but he did care about the people who spoke foreign tongues, he made a park and a stage for music with a tall pole in the middle of the park and many ropes to form a star that fell from the tall post to other shorter posts and he had white flutter paper strung all over the ropes and letters that said "San Felipe, My Magical Town," and people from far away took photographs with him on his stage and he invited them to the town hall. He didn't know who the musician in white was, but he saw in the newspaper that he was known in other tongues and he sent one of his messengers from the government to ask me to tell him when famous artists came to see me.

There was a road already and there were streets that the governor made for the foreigners when Paloma went to the city and loved a man with a sickness still unborn in him, a man who carried the sickness that sang to her death's trill.

18

My mother called my father to tell him they'd kicked Leandra out of her third school for starting a fire. She'd tried several times to call Leandra's cell phone, but Leandra hadn't picked up. My father didn't talk to Leandra until a few days later, when he asked her to explain what had happened.

A woman named Micaela had been working at the school since its founding twenty years earlier. She was the single mother of a thirteen-year-old in my sister's class. Cuauhtémoc had studied there on a full scholarship since preschool, on two conditions: Micaela's continued employment at the school and his grade point average. Cuauhtémoc was shy and didn't speak up in class unless the teacher called on him. Over time, it just became the norm that he didn't interact with his classmates and his classmates didn't interact with him. No one bothered him; some ignored his presence, others said hello but never went beyond the bare minimum. They never invited him to their houses or their parties. He'd gone on one field trip and helped with the preparations for their middle school graduation, but that was all.

Cuauhtémoc seemed to have a whole separate life. He didn't need his classmates, and they didn't need him. He had one friend at school, a short kid a year below him with a knack for coding. Cuauhtémoc wasn't interested in the same things as other teenagers. He wasn't interested in fitting in with them or being part of their conversations and he wasn't interested in girls yet. He was tall, much taller than his mother. He wore hand-knitted sweaters, polyester trousers, and T-shirts with references that none of his classmates understood; when I first met him, he was wearing a brown scarf his mother had knitted for him.

Leandra got along with Cuauhtémoc from the minute she arrived at the school. She chatted with him and sat next to him in class, they established a friendship, and – in part because of my sister's nature and in part because of his personality – Leandra became a bridge between him and her other new friends at the school.

One of those new friends was a girl from a Catholic family whose parents had recently divorced; the girl's father was a notary and had a country house that Leandra began to hear epic stories about. A bunch of her classmates had gone there and had a blast, except for the one who got appendicitis. She said the house was nuts, there was a place to build bonfires and a home cinema with a popcorn machine and everything, and blankets on each seat. The mother got the country house in the divorce and started using it more often with her only daughter. They went every weekend they could, and they brought friends. The daughter had thrown a party at the country house a little while before Leandra arrived at the school; she'd invited a few classmates and her mother had brought a few people and some of the couples had teenage kids who joined in with her daughter's friends.

Leandra, Cuauhtémoc, and his friend were sitting around in a circle, talking with a few of the kids who had been there. They'd brought a joint and had smoked it somewhere in the house; later, they'd made a film. That's what they called it, at least – they'd assigned themselves roles and everything but, in reality, it was a string of inside jokes interrupted by attacks of uncontrollable laughter. They screened it later in the home film cinema. A few of the adults watched a bit of it, but they got bored quickly and left the teenagers alone in front of the screen. In the middle of telling the group what the film was about, the girl gave in to a rush of enthusiasm and invited everyone present to her country house, including Leandra, Cuauhtémoc, and his friend from the year below them.

The girl spoke with her mother and told her that she'd invited some people out to the country house the following weekend, including two new friends she'd made at school, Leandra and Cuauhtémoc. Her mother didn't know who Leandra was, but she'd seen Cuauhtémoc in her daughter's class photo year after year; she knew that he was the son of the woman who cleaned the bathrooms at the school and might even have found his name charming. She'd heard that Micaela was previously employed by the school's founder, who'd sold his interest years earlier, and she had greeted her once, purely by coincidence, at an open-air festival. She was fairly certain there was only one student at the school named Cuauhtémoc, and when she asked her daughter if she was talking about the boy whose mother was a janitor, she said yes. The woman completely lost it and went to the school the next day to speak with the director. They met behind closed doors, rumours began to circulate, and then two or three days later Cuauhtémoc was gone.

Leandra spoke with Micaela. She told her they'd revoked Cuauhtémoc's scholarship because his grades had slipped, which was true, though they were still pretty close to the terms of their agreement with the school. The director had used a technicality to kick him out, hiding behind it like a shield. Micaela knew what had really happened and didn't want a fight. She knew that the girl's mother had thrown a fit because she couldn't stand the thought of paying all that tuition, of donating money for the construction of a new chemistry lab and an annexe for the lower school, just to have her daughter spending time with the children of the help. The school didn't have all its papers in order and had just spent a fortune on that annexe, and the director didn't want any trouble with the girl's family, who had notarised, pro bono, all the paperwork. The director had run out of resources, but no one needed to know that. The simplest path was to kick Cuauhtémoc out and get the girl's mother off her back, protecting the daily operations of the school. After that conversation with Micaela in the bathroom, my sister slipped a small can of gas from the chemistry lab into her backpack, pulled out her Zippo Spectrum, and set fire to the dumpster behind the school buses.

The flames licked the fiberglass roof that covered part of the dumpster and the branches above it began to sway from the heat. Soon, those began to burn, as well. The fire threatened to spread to through the trees to the buses and nearby cars, but by the time the leaves were beginning to catch, a few students had already begun to gather. Between them, three bus drivers, a chemistry teacher, and the father of a student who'd arrived early to pick him up, they managed to contain the fire with a hose, a few buckets of water, and the night watchman's blankets. But without fire extinguishers.

The mother of one of the third-year students, who worked at a law firm, heard what happened and called the director. How could the facilities be so unsafe? Her son had told her that they didn't even have fire extinguishers.

That same afternoon the director received a request to produce proof of the school's compliance with safety regulations in case of fire or earthquake. The director was furious, and told my mother over the phone that Thank God they'd been able to control the fire, that of course there were fire extinguishers at the school but Leandra had put everyone's life at risk. My parents found out later that Leandra had known the fire extinguishers were expired, and that if anyone was going to be hurt by a fire in that specific area of the school, it was going to be the director. So she picked a time, took her shot, and hit the bullseye.

My father punished Leandra, but they struck a deal. He went to the school to speak with the director about Cuauhtémoc, and told her that he and my mother with their two jobs had the privilege of being able to send Leandra to another school, and that he expected Micaela's years of hard work should guarantee her the same privilege of being able to offer an education to her child, that is, unless the director wanted to find herself in the middle of a discrimination lawsuit.

The school closed for two weeks. The director and her administrative team managed to get the institution's paperwork in order, purchase new fire extinguishers, and get government approval on the emergency exits and earthquake contingency plan. The deal Leandra cut with my father accomplished what she had wanted to do by confronting the director, though she'd done it like a thirteen-year-old hungry for attention. My father cornered the director into an agreement: there would be no lawsuit as long as Cuauhtémoc was allowed back.

Leandra was grounded for two months. One of the few exceptions my parents made, which was actually more of a request on their part, was having her invite Cuauhtémoc over for dinner. They wanted to meet him. They knew it was important to punish her for what she'd done, but it seemed more important to make sure that Leandra never set another fire, that she never put herself or anyone else at risk, ever again.

My own fire came late.

Feliciana offered me three ceremonies. She reminded me again that Paloma had brought me to San Felipe because I had unfinished business. In her hut when night fell, she pulled out a small calabash cup full of a black powder that she spread on my forearms. The powder also covered her hands and she began to sing a simple melody that sounded like the songs children invent when they play. As she sang, she walked slowly around me in a circle, losing herself; with a gesture, she told me to lick the black powder from her hands, and kept singing. It tasted like earth and lead. A few seconds later, I vomited and she squatted beside me, comforting me and I understood from her that it was part of the ceremony. Her song was melodic, rhythmic; she repeated certain words, alternating and changing them like a kaleidoscope of sounds, the way children play with the words they've just learned.

She held a piece of silk dyed red by her daughter Apolonia. She pulled the mushrooms from it, brushed the dirt off them with her fingers, and gave me three pairs. She ate three, as well. They tasted a lot like the mushrooms we buy at the supermarket. After eating them I suddenly felt hot. I took off my jacket while Feliciana walked around me again slowly, singing a phrase she made small variations to, creating new images with the sound. Feliciana took my hand in hers, and when I felt her skin against mine it was like we'd both begun to float. We drifted up and out of her hut through the wooden door. We soared over the milpa and over San Felipe. I saw the town far below me, its lights fading into the distance the way they look from an aeroplane window at take-off, blinking smaller and smaller. I saw the immensity of the night sky. And I realised that Feliciana wasn't with me anymore. I rose faster and faster into space and way up there I saw blurry particles in different shades of grey like organisms moving under a microscope, unstable pixels. Suddenly I was moving again; descending, returning. I saw my way back clearly until I passed through the white clouds hanging in the night sky, then I saw the small blinking lights of San Felipe, the mountains, a cane field nearby, the milpa and an electrical line that crossed the gully under my feet, the thatched roof of Feliciana's hut, the wooden door I opened, the chair I was sitting in and my hand, which Feliciana touched as she sang. This time the contact with her skin sent me inside her hand on a journey just as long as the one I'd taken into space and just as perfect in its geometry; I travelled into the furthest reaches of her body, all the way inside a cell, to the furthest depths I could reach. There I saw blurry particles in different shades of grey like organisms under a microscope, unstable pixels at the deepest point of my journey identical to what I had seen at the highest point as I travelled through the milky way, and even though Felix didn't physically appear, I knew that the journey was my son.

Feliciana asked me to return each of the next two nights. The second night, she performed a ceremony with the Language. I lay down on a mat next to her altar, which was lit by candles the colour of milky coffee. I lay down on some herbs that Feliciana had gone to the hillside to cut for me that afternoon. She asked me a few questions, my interpreter guided us. Feliciana described to me the images that were coming to her, and how they complemented what I was saying. I understood that the space my father had created in the garage for doing what he loved was also a message for the two of us, and I understood that, unlike my sister, I still had unfinished business there. In my role as firstborn, I hadn't allowed myself to do what I wanted – I'd always done what I thought I should do. My responsibilities at the newspaper had made me forget why I wanted to study journalism in the first place, which was the same reason I signed up for drum lessons and wrote poetry curled up in my single bed.

Feliciana guided me to a scene from my childhood I'd never given any thought to, one I didn't even remember, but that emerged from underneath other memories as my first moment of complicity with my father. We were watching television; he was holding the remote and was flipping between channels. I was around five. Something happened in a film we'd begun watching in the middle, and we both started to laugh. The fact that there was nothing particularly funny about what was on the screen only made us laugh harder and harder. Lying there on the mat, I began to laugh. On the third night, Feliciana gave me four pairs of mushrooms and guided me with the Language, she read me a page from the Book. This is yours, she said, this is your page and these words of the Language are yours, Zoe. This is the page you were missing.

19

There are different types of mushrooms. The ones that grow in the dung of cattle, we call those Oxen, because they grow together like two beasts yoked to the plough. The ones that grow on the trees during the rains, we call those mushrooms Cats. We call the ones that grow in the cane fields Birds and the ones that grow in the moist earth of the hillside Children. The mushrooms I gave you were Children, those are the ones I use in my ceremonies. I've also used Cats but they are not as powerful as Children, they're like cats and only come to you if they want, otherwise they stay in the tree where they grew even as you chew them, they stay there in the tree and you never know when they will come to you, or if they will come to you or not, will they be purring if they appear or will they stay in the tree where they grew, scratching the bark on the trunk where you picked them. Cats join the ceremony when they want, if they want, but if they do join, they come purring. Birds are similar but those are sheer, Birds are sheer like dreams are light in the day before they fly from us, dreams are sheer in the day like wings that are light to fly. Oxen are powerful only if you eat several pairs, the same way a team of oxen must bring together the strength of many to till the soil and those you have to guide, you have to tell them, come this way but not over there, and then yes, here. Children are the present, they are the most powerful because they are the present and just as vast as the present are the visions they bring. People say the present lasts only as long as a word because with the next word the other one is already past, one is always right on the tail of the other, people say to me what are these visions if the present does not last, and I say the present is as vast as the person and it is as vast as the Language.

In the ceremony I made for Guadalupe where I saw how his father looked at him in his tunic the flame orange of a fire in the night and how he laughed at him from far away, I saw how Children heal the soul and not only the sick body because they see the present as vast as it is, the present is not only the present of the body. Children don't tell the future, it is the Language that shines its sun on the present, that illuminates its vastness. I saw this clearly with Guadalupe, as clear as the morning brings clear the trillings of birds I saw it when they brought Guadalupe to me and I healed the sickness he carried in his soul from his father. The mushrooms we call Children are powerful, they tell the truth and their present hides no shadows, they look into the deep waters of the present with the Language that shines its sun, and that is why people say to me, Feliciana, you see the future, but I tell them no, I see the present. And sometimes the past and the future wander through the sufferings of the body and the soul and they appear to me, and so people say, Feliciana, you see the future, but if it appears it is because the future is wandering through the present. The mushrooms we call Children don't under-stand what is past, they don't understand what is future, they don't know what is yesterday or tomorrow, they don't care. They live in the present like children do.

I've healed elders and I've healed children, and a child is more easily healed. A child is lighter to heal than a man because the man drowns in the deep waters of his woes, he drowns in the deep waters of his dark sorrows, but the child with fevers that boil his blood and icy sweats that won't let him sleep, that child smiles at the man who gives him a glass of water because that glass of water remedies his present because the child is not drowning in his woes, he has no deep waters and no dark sorrows, the child is clear water, and not even with fevers that boil his blood or icy sweats that won't let him sleep, not even then does he think about what will happen the next day or how he suffered, because the child is clear water, it is his family that suffers more, his relatives carry more sorrow than the sick child. The child is not afraid of the past or of the future, the child is not afraid of death. Children do not understand death, say the word death to a child and you will see he has no knowledge of the egg death lays in people. Man is afraid of death's egg and when he falls sick his sorrows fall on him heavy and they bury him with their heaviness, if the sickness is light he says, I won't be able to work tomorrow, and if the sickness is heavy he says, I won't be able to work the day after tomorrow, and if he has fevers he is afraid that death laid its egg in him. I say to them, what is missing for you, why are you afraid, why are people afraid of what the future brings them, why do you carry the past, I say, what is missing for you today, you have feet and hands, you have air to breathe and water to drink, you have earth to walk on, food to eat and fire to warm it up, you have your life, you have everything. I have my life and I have everything. I tell you, when I die I'll come right back here to my hut in San Felipe and my ceremonies and the food my sister Francisca makes and I'll ask her to make me atole because what we have here is good, and so I say to people, What is missing for you, if you have everything, if you have everything today nothing will be missing tomorrow.

The mushrooms we call Children are wise because wise is the Language. Wise is the voice, not the body, just as God reaches us not in body but in voice, and of that voice is the Language He used to make us and to give us all things. People in town said the mushrooms spoke English from all the foreigners who came to see me in San Felipe. I speak only my tongue, this tongue that reaches you through an interpreter, this tongue that is the tongue of my ancestors. I will not end my tongue with Spanish, I will not end my tongue with any other because this tongue is who I am, it is the tongue of my ancestors and this tongue made me who I am, I honour who I am when I speak it.

Paloma went to the city and came back with a sickness still unborn but about to be and one day she said to me, Feliciana, she said, I slipped away from Guadalupe at night, love, I slipped away from San Felipe, I slipped away from the fate of being Gaspar, but I can't slip away from death, I have a sickness still unborn in me and it won't be what takes me, but it will be the reason I go. Death had already laid its egg in her, first when she became Paloma and loved a politician, then when she loved a loveless man and his lovelessness left her beaten. Paloma with her sickness still unborn went with another man here in San Felipe and she gave the sickness to him without knowing she had it, and in his rage about what Paloma had given him in their nights, in his rage that man killed Paloma with a dagger in her back. When I saw her room, when I saw her body and her bed and her peacock blanket I remembered what my grandfather Cosme said about Paloma when she was still the boy Gaspar, he said that Gaspar walked like he had feathers. I tell you, those words of rage from my grandfather Cosme said to death, Lay your egg here.

Paloma once said to me, she said, Feliciana, love, the ones who leave this earth on God's time go at six in the morning, the ones who leave by the hand of man go at six at night, because death sang as clear as the sun shines to Paloma that death was coming to her at six at night and when Guadalupe came to tell me they killed her with the shine on her hands I went to her house and saw Paloma twice in the mirror and both times she looked so alive except for the stain of blood spreading out from under her where she had the hole they made in her with a dagger. It was six at night, I know it was six because she told me it would be, and the shadows were falling there across the milpa. I don't know times, I don't know dates, I don't know when I was born so don't ask me that because I don't know, but I know that terrible hour. It was exactly six at night because the light cast shadows on the milpa and I saw her and I knew that man had killed her with a dagger in her back from his rage at Paloma for being Muxe, he killed her for being Muxe, he killed her because she was born a man and lived as a woman, he killed her because she wore the dresses and shine that women wear, as if killing Paloma could relieve him like the rains relieve the clouds fat with summer's heat, the wretch killed Paloma for his rage that she was Muxe, that she gave him a disease still unborn, and so they killed Paloma for being Muxe, they killed her for being a woman, they killed her for being a curandera, because people often mistake lovelessness for love, and so they killed her and at six at night the Language left me, and I stayed that way because what need do I have for the Words without Paloma. My grandson Aparicio brought them back to me later with a sickness I needed to cure, but the Language dried up again in me when I saw shadows fall again across the milpa and knew again that they had killed Paloma, I was emptied of the Words and I was left like a dried well.

Say this, say all of what I'm saying to you. Say that it was six at night when Guadalupe came to tell me they killed Paloma. Say what you saw and what I told you, honour what you say, honour what your father said to you just as I honour what mine said to me, honour your work with the Language just as I honour my father Felisberto with what he gave me, honour what your mother said to you just as I honour what mine said to me, honour your ancestors with the Language because the present is of them, honour your sister just as I honour my sister Francisca and my sister Paloma who gave me back the Book in my dreams because she knew it had left me, I saw her with her sparkles giving it to me so I could heal my grandson Aparicio. Tell your story and tell mine because they are not two stories but one, this is why I asked you over and over about yours. Say your name or say my name or say both, your name is mine and they are the same because high and low we are all the same, it doesn't matter what name you say, yours or mine because we are all children of the Language, we all come from the Language and when we die we return to it, just like Paloma is here with me every day talking to me the way she talked. She is my Language now. She is here with me as I speak to you, she speaks to you through my words. You visited your deep waters and saw, your deep waters tell you not what your name is but why your name is yours, they tell you this voice is yours, your deep waters tell you, Here is where I begin and where the others end because here is where your Language begins, the Language that belongs to you and no one else. The one you will now write.

AUTHOR'S NOTE

I'd like to offer special thanks to my brother Diego, my sister-in-law Simmone and their children Kai and Uma. To my family. Many thanks to Gabriela Jáuregui, Elena Fortes, Luis Felipe Fabre, Mauro Libertella, Juan Cárdenas, Guillermo Núñez Jáuregui, Verónica Gerber, Amalia Pica. To Juan Andrés Gaitán, Gabriel Kahan, Vera Félix, Federico Schott, Tania Pérez Córdova, Francesco Pedraglio, Eduardo Omas, Nina Hoechtl, Julieta Venegas, Tania Lili, Valeria Luiselli, Lydia Cacho, Vivian Abenshushan, Elvira Liceaga, Laura Gandol, Mariana Barrera, José Terán, Samanta Schweblin, Julia Reyes Retana, Amalia Andrade, to my cherished Redtenters, to Lourdes Valdés (I am and always will be grateful to you). To Pedro de Tavira. To Claudio López Lamadrid RIP and my grandmother Gloria RIP. To Pilar Reyes, Mayra González, Fernanda Álvarez and Paz Balmaceda at Alfaguara; to Carina Pons and Jorge Manzanilla at the Balcells agency: how incredibly lucky I am to work with you all.

I wrote this book thanks to a grant from the SNC.

TRANSLATOR'S NOTE

No matter how simple it might appear at first glance, every translation is thick with linguistic choices that carry political and aesthetic implications. Some of these choices – like leaving certain culturally specific terms in the language of the original – are immediately visible; some others are not.

Some terms, for example, demand to be left in their original form; these are often described as "untranslatables". Words like hyggelig, yakamoz, and Schadenfreude invite us to engage with other worldviews and think beyond familiar notions of, say, coziness, moonlight and misanthropy; they invite us to connect across and through the difference we see before us. Literary translation is also warming to untranslatables. This change was facilitated by the ready access most readers now have to internet search engines, but its implications extend beyond the technological: it also has a political dimension. While there's no one-size-fits-all answer for any question of translation, the choice not to translate these culturally dense terms asserts that not everything should be easy or crystal clear in the target language, as this sense of clarity is so often won through the violence of erasure. This is especially true when translating into a hegemonic language.

Take, for example, the milpa where several key scenes from Feliciana's narrative occur. The word "milpa" is derived from the Nahuatl and refers both to the parcel of land where corn, beans and squash are cultivated alongside complementary crops, and to the traditional techniques of farming employed on that parcel to promote biodiversity and avoid exhausting the soil. The milpa, then, is not only a key source of food; it represents an intergenerational philosophy based on establishing balance between land, crops, community, and tradition. In other words, a milpa is not a cornfield; to translate it as such would efface this millenary agricultural practice and replace it with mirages of the Midwest.

Similarly, a güero is not simply a blonde. While the term certainly applies to a person with blonde hair, it is used more broadly – sometimes as a term of endearment – to indicate any light-skinned individual. In the mountains of Oaxaca, in an Indigenous community affected by colonial violence and racist state policies, this is more than merely a visual marker. It is an indication of otherness even when applied fondly, as it is when Feliciana describes the linguistically adept but culturally clueless graduate student who comes to her village as an interpreter after her healing ceremonies bring her international fame. It is certainly a mark of otherness when she uses it to describe the European academics who want her to travel across the ocean and speak in crowded lecture halls about her use of entheogenic mushrooms.

The list goes on. In recognition of both its cultural specificity and the novel's sustained reflection on gender norms and the violence that attends them, I left the term "curandera" (curandero when it refers to a person who identifies as male) in Spanish. The question of gender as it relates to the title of traditional healer is central to the novel's plot: after discovering that her path is to follow in the footsteps of the men in her family, a line of respected curanderos, Feliciana has to contend with the discrimination of her family and the broader community because, according to tradition, women cannot perform the mushroom ceremonies known as veladas. Losing the gendered ending of curandera would have obscured this key aspect of the text.

It was likewise important to keep "bruja" and its masculine counterpart, "brujo", in Spanish (as much as possible). Because the title of the book is *Witches*, the term needed to appear in the body of the text in English, as well, but it was essential to maintain a trace of the original usage for two principal reasons: for the difference in status between a brujo/a and the much more respected curandero/a, and also because, despite its apparent translatability, "bruja" does not map exactly onto "witch". A bruja might literally traffic in spells, but the term can also be used figuratively to dismiss a woman as a nag; this is true in English as well, but it is far less common these days. On the other hand, a woman with a highly developed sense of intuition might admiringly be called a bruja (this polysemy does not apply to the masculine form). It is precisely the contradictory figurative uses of the label as it is applied to women that serves as the conceptual axis of this novel. *Witches* is an exploration of the many ways that women and gender non-conforming individuals are marginalised in our hetero-normative patriarchy. It is also a celebration of the bonds they forge and of alternative ways of knowing.

Then there are the less obviously politically charged, but no less culturally specific, terms – as a picture is worth a thousand words, I do recommend looking these up as a supplement to this commentary. There is clothing, including traditional embroidered huipiles and tehuanas, and the iconic shoes known as huaraches made from woven leather straps; foodstuffs like atole, a hearty drink made with corn flour and served warm. And, of course, pulque – an unfiltered alcoholic drink made from fermented maguey that dates back to pre-Hispanic times, when it was a sacred beverage. Pulque is pulque, just like grappa is grappa and sake is sake, and if the time hasn't yet arrived when rendering the beverage in English would seem as unnecessary as translating sake into "Japanese rice wine", it surely won't be long. By extension, the pulquería Feliciana mentions in her memories of her father would have been a traditional watering hole where people would gather to drink pulque; we get a sense of the state's negligence of Feliciana's community in her observation that between San Felipe, the town she moved to after her father died and which was later "swallowed by the city", and San Juan de los Lagos, the village where she grew up, there were six pulquerías but no schoolhouse.

The festive velas that Paloma loves to dress up for are Muxe celebration-pageants where drinking and dancing go on far into the night. Paloma herself is Muxe, a third gender recognised among the Zapotec peoples in Oaxaca; she was named Gaspar at birth and raised as male in the family tradition of curanderos, but experienced increasing emotional and physical violence as she distanced herself from masculine gender norms. The vela is etymologically connected – by way of the candle, also *vela* – to the velada, a term I ultimately chose to leave in Spanish only once. This single instance is meant to carry the term's rich history into the text and also, through its placement, to highlight the connection between the pageants, Feliciana's ceremonies, and the velorio or wake held after Paloma's murder, which I translated as "vigil" to capture as much as I could of the resonance between these three very distinct kinds of rituals.

In all these cases, I made the – visible – choice not to translate certain terms in recognition of the specificity of the practices and objects described in the text. There was, however, an upper limit to how much I could leave in Spanish. Because the novel is written as two first-person accounts – one, the product of a recorded interview that has already gone through a process of translation (interpretation, really) into Spanish – the language needed to flow naturally and the intimacy of the conversation needed to come across. It wouldn't do to overemphasise the foreignness of the text or to pull the reader out of the narrative by leaving too many terms in any given passage in Spanish. These decisions ultimately draw on a combination of instinct, experience and research, as artistic choices so often do.

This is where the less visible part of the translation comes in.

Readers familiar with the cultural history of Mexico and/or the cultural history of psilocybin might have sensed something familiar in the story of a woman of indeterminate age living somewhere in the mountains of Mexico and performing ritual healing ceremonies with entheogenic mushrooms she refers to as "Children". Such a woman did, in fact, exist: her name was María Sabina Magdalena García and she was a Mazatec curandera born in Huautla de Jiménez in the state of Oaxaca toward the end of the nineteenth century. She lived through the Mexican Revolution; she married, bore children, was widowed, and then dedicated her life to traditional healing. A banker and his wife did travel from New York to participate in one of her sacred mushroom ceremonies and wrote about her for *Life* magazine in 1957; she was later immortalised on film and sought after by prominent artists of the 1960s. As a result of all this attention – for bringing waves of foreigners to her mountain village, for sharing millenary rituals with güeros – María Sabina was ostracised from her community, threatened, and persecuted by the Mexican police. Her home was burned to the ground. She also became an international icon and, in her way, a prominent defender of women's and Indigenous rights.

To be clear, *Witches* is not biographical or historical fiction, but one of its central characters does bear a striking resemblance to a person who inhabited this planet for a time, a person who left an archive after she passed. And so, just as Lozano draws inspiration for her novel from certain details of María Sabina's life, I used certain details of María Sabina's physical and linguistic gestures to anchor my translation. Particularly useful was the video footage I was able to find of the renowned curandera: the flickers of mischief in her unflinching gaze, the cigarettes she took such pleasure in smoking, the trainers she wore under her traditional dress; the rhythms of her speech and the way she looked, or not, at her interlocutor as she spoke. I also perused existing translations of her chants and descriptions of her ceremonies in English. I did not follow the model of these materials literally – Lozano's approach to this figure is elliptical, so mine needed to be, too – but I wanted to engage them just enough that some of the resonances that would strike a reader in Mexico from, say, a demographic similar to Zoe's, would at least be traceable back to this root in English.

Thinking about the multiple processes of triangulation at work in this novel, as well as in its writing and translation, I couldn't help but imagine the processes of triangulation involved in its reception in this new cultural and linguistic context. And to hope that Zoe and Feliciana's exchange of stories will offer to the readers of *Witches* a chance to connect across and through difference.

Heather Cleary
New York, November 2021

BRENDA LOZANO is a fiction writer, essayist and editor. Born in Mexico City, she studied literature in Mexico and the United States. She has participated in literary residencies in the US, Europe and Latin America, and her work has appeared in several anthologies, including *Mexico20* and *Bogotá39*. She edits the literary journal *Make* in Chicago and is part of Ugly Duckling Presse in New York. She is the author of two earlier novels, *Todo nada* (2009), which is currently being adapted for the screen, and *Cuaderno Ideal* (2015), recently published by Charco Press in an English translation by Annie McDermott as *Loop*, and a book of short stories, *Cómo piensan las piedras* (2017). In 2015, she was recognised by Conaculta, the Hay Festival and the British Council as one of the most important authors under forty years of age from Mexico, and in 2017 she was selected by the Hay Festival for *Bogotá 39*, a list of the most outstanding new authors from Latin America. She currently lives in Mexico City.

HEATHER CLEARY is a translator and writer based in New York and Mexico City. She holds an MA in Comparative Literature from NYU and a PhD in Latin American and Iberian Cultures from Columbia University, and teaches at Sarah Lawrence College. Her essays and literary criticism have appeared in *Two Lines*, *Lit Hub* and *Words Without Borders*, among other publications, and her book, *The Translator's Visibility: Scenes from Contemporary Latin American Fiction*, is forthcoming from Bloomsbury. Her translations include work by Betina González, María Ospina, Mario Bellatin, Roque Larraquy, Sergio Chejfec and a selection of Girondo's poetry, *Poems to Read on a Streetcar*, published by New Directions. She lives in New York City.